The Perfect Blend

WELCOME TO REDEMPTION, BOOK 3

DONNA MARIE ROGERS

The Perfect Blend
Copyright © 2011 Donna Marie Rogers
First Published 2007 by The Wild Rose Press

Excerpt from *Grounds for Change* © 2011 Stacey Joy Netzel

ISBN: 978-1-941829-08-0
Published by Donna Kowalczyk
Contact Information: www.DonnaMarieRogers.com

Cover Design: The Killion Group, Inc.
Interior Formatting: Author E.M.S.

Published in the United States of America.

Jamie, this one's for you.

Praise for Donna Marie Rogers

THAT MAGIC TOUCH

"Sheer genius. I will now put all future books by this author on my must read list."

—5 Stars, Amazon Reviewer

THERE'S ONLY BEEN YOU

"Love lost and found is the basis of this wonderfully heartwarming read. Throw in a years-old lie and a strong sense of family and it only gets better and better."

—4 Stars, RT Book Reviews

"Readers of contemporary romance will be thoroughly delighted...Donna Marie Rogers delivers a tender tale of love, family, and second chances."

—5 Bookmarks, Wild on Books

MEANT TO BE

"The plot kept me spellbound throughout the entire book. Rogers has the ability to keep her readers on the edge of our seats."

—5 Hearts, The Romance Studio

"The material is tightly written, well plotted and fast paced, and the characters are unforgettable."

—5 Books, Long and Short Reviews

WELCOME TO REDEMPTION SERIES

"With their easy, breezy style and skilled characterizations, Rogers and Netzel have created a town that readers won't want to leave."

—4½ Stars – RT Book Reviews

Donna Marie Rogers' Titles

LAKE SHELBYVILLE SERIES
That Magic Touch

JAMISON FAMILY SERIES
There's Only Been You
Foolish Pride
Meant To Be

DOUBLE M RANCH SERIES
Golden Opportunity
Golden Dream

WELCOME TO REDEMPTION SERIES
(small town romance series with Stacey Joy Netzel)
A Fair of the Heart (Book 1)
The Perfect Blend (Book 3)
Home Is Where the Heart Is (Book 5)
Never Let Me Go (Book 7)
Say You Love Me (Book 9)

Chapter One

"You know, you could turn this place into a real success with just a few minor changes."

Carrie Lowell shot a quick frown up from the espresso she was brewing. She did a double take when she realized the deep voice doling out business advice belonged to the hottie who worked across the street at the library.

"Excuse me?"

"Add some books and magazines, expand the menu to include sandwiches and wraps, maybe stay open 'til five. The cheese factory lets out at three thirty so—"

"Uh, Matt, right?" At his nod, she said, "Look, don't take this the wrong way, but you're a librarian. If I needed advice on which new novel to check out, your word would be gold. Get my drift?" She handed her customer the cappuccino she'd just made. "Want it on your tab, Bill?"

"Yep. Thanks, Care."

Once Bill left, Matt said, "See? How do you expect to keep this place afloat when you don't even charge your customers for their orders?"

Carrie turned to face him, hands on hips. She couldn't believe the freakin' librarian was standing here giving her business advice. "Not that it's any of your concern, *Matt*, but I'm doing just fine. Now go file books away or something and leave me be." She made a shooing motion with her hands.

Matt crossed his arms across his chest and peered at her over his glasses. It struck her that she'd never thought a man could look sexy in glasses, but somehow Matt rocked his. Yeah, he was a hottie all right. Big whiskey-brown eyes, thick, dark blond hair with sun-kissed highlights. Tall, slim, but with broad shoulders and lean muscled arms. She'd bet he looked damn good in a pair of swim trunks—

"I'm not a child, Ms. Lowell, and since I happen to be your only paying customer, I wouldn't be so quick to dismiss me if I were you."

"Which you're not." She crossed her own arms over her chest—which wasn't quite as effective with her boobs in the way, making it look more like she was imitating *I Dream of Jeannie*. "Me, that is. So mind your own business."

He smiled suddenly, displaying perfectly white, straight teeth. "You're like a five-year-old who doesn't like to be told what to do."

Was this guy for real? She slapped her hands down on the counter. "Who the hell do you think you are?"

"Matt Jacobs—"

"It was a rhetorical question."

"—and I happen to have a business degree, so would it really kill you to listen to me?"

Well, la-di-freakin'-da. "Why do you even care? My God, we barely know each other, and within the space of two minutes you've offered me unwanted business advice *and* insulted me. My closest friends wouldn't dare speak to me the way you have."

He cocked a brow. "Maybe that's part of the problem. You need someone to give it to you straight."

"Uh-huh. And you're just the man for the job, right? Please."

"Maybe I am." He let out a sigh and swiped his fingers through his hair. "Look, even a blind man could see how poor your business has been the past few months—"

"It's summer!"

"—and I know you could turn it around with some fairly simple changes and longer hours."

"I think you need to leave now."

He plucked at his sky blue, short-sleeved, button collar shirt and frowned as he glanced around. "It's warm in here. Don't you have the air on?"

Carrie's cheeks flamed. The air-conditioner had conked out over the weekend, and she couldn't afford to replace it right now. Heck, she could barely afford to keep her doors open at this point. Maybe she needed to swallow her pride and take on a partner, like that new boyfriend of Tara's suggested. The guy seemed certain that selling half of her shop would solve her problems. Well, except one—Carrie didn't like to share. But an influx of cash was about the only thing that would save this place right now. And maybe someone with a little business sense.

"It broke down this morning," she lied, too embarrassed to admit the truth. "I haven't had a chance to have it serviced yet."

"I could take a look at it, if you'd like." He smiled, transforming his boyishly handsome face into one that made her pulse leap.

She wanted to kiss him. She hadn't wanted to kiss a man in almost three years, and here she was, aching to pull him down and lay one on him. She cleared her throat, grabbed a washrag, and went to town on the counter. Had to keep those hands busy. "Thanks, but I'd rather leave it to the experts." She chanced a peek up at him.

His smile faded. "Suit yourself."

"I will."

"Fine."

"*Fine.*" She met his gaze, not caring how childish she sounded.

He mumbled something that included the words "stubborn" and "idiot," then strode out the door.

"Good riddance," Carrie snapped as the bell tinkled in his wake. Good riddance? *Sheesh, great comeback, Care.* She leaned against the counter and pouted, watching as he crossed the street and disappeared into the library. Well, he was right about one thing: she was as stubborn as a mule. And when it came to men, the word 'idiot' wasn't far off either.

"I swear, the woman's nuts," Matt griped, glowering out the window. "And mean as a snake. You'd think she'd appreciate my input. Appreciate that I cared enough to walk into her shop and—"

"Tell her how to run her business?" Caleb Hunter set his books and library card on the counter. "Yeah, it's amazing she didn't melt at your feet."

"You're just sticking up for her 'cause she's your girlfriend's best friend."

Caleb grinned. "There is that."

Matt tore his gaze away from the infuriating woman—who was busy cleaning windows—to checkout Caleb's books. A smile lifted his lips when he scanned in the first one. "For Emma?"

"No, I thought I'd read *Green Eggs and Ham* to Lauren tonight. Dr. Seuss is a surprising turn-on for her."

Matt burst out laughing. "Smartass. Could've been for Max."

"Actually, the book on hotwiring a car is for Max."

"Someone's in fine form today." Matt handed Caleb back his library card. "So, we still on for supper?"

"You bet. Lauren's making mostaccioli, fresh-baked Italian bread, and cheesecake for dessert."

Matt grinned. Lauren was an excellent cook, and if Caleb wasn't careful, he'd have a Buddha belly in no time. "Hundred bucks says you'll need a new wardrobe by Halloween."

Caleb patted his stomach. "Nah, I just have to learn to pace myself. See you later, man."

"Later." A twinge of envy tightened Matt's chest. He'd had so few home-cooked meals in his life; he couldn't even imagine what it would feel like to have a woman cook a meal for him. In his world, you either dined out or ordered takeout. A visual of Carrie slaving over a hot stove made him snort out loud. Crazy woman would more likely serve him up as the main entrée. Trussed up in a pan with an apple in his mouth. He rolled his eyes. At least he wouldn't have to think about her for the rest of the night.

His cell phone rang. Matt dug it out of his front pocket and let out a sigh when he saw the caller ID. "Hey, Lindy, what's up?"

"Dad's in the hospital," his baby sister replied, her tone cool.

Matt collapsed onto the chair. "My God, what happened?"

"He had a heart attack. Last night."

"And you're just calling me now?"

"He...It was pretty late. And it was a mild attack, so Mom didn't see any reason to bother you."

Matt squeezed his eyes shut. His mother didn't think he'd give a damn. Big difference.

"Matt? I have to go. I'll keep you informed, okay?"

"Thanks. Give Dad—tell him to take care of himself."

"I will. Talk to you soon."

He ended the call with a heavy heart. Guilt gnawed at him until he wanted to put his fist through the goddamn wall. If he'd just stayed and taken over the company reins so the old man could retire, his parents would be sipping piña coladas in the Caribbean right now. Instead, his father was lying in a hospital bed while his mother no doubt worried herself sick.

Thanks to their only son.

By the time four o'clock rolled around, Matt wasn't much in the mood for socializing. Maybe he'd swing past Lauren's to say hi before heading home. Then maybe he'd pack his bags and head to L.A., see for himself that his father was all right. And, hell, maybe he'd stay. After today, he was fairly certain he didn't have a future in Redemption anyway. The one woman who heated his blood could barely remember his name. Yep, he'd made some impression on Ms. Carrie Lowell, hadn't he?

Matt pulled into Lauren's driveway and killed the engine. He sat for a minute, hands clutching the steering wheel, as he debated whether or not to stay for supper. He was torn, especially if this turned out to be the last meal he shared with these two. In just a few short months, Caleb Hunter had become one of the best friends he'd ever had. And Lauren Frazier was a dream: sweet, generous, funny, a great mom. A real home and hearth type.

Thank God neither of them knew what a damn fraud he was.

"Hey, you daydreaming or what?" Caleb said as he smacked the hood and scared the hell out of him. "Come on, I got an ice-cold Bud waiting for you."

Matt shook his head as he climbed out of the old Jeep Wrangler he'd purchased on his first day in town. The cheapest vehicle he'd ever owned, and by far his favorite. "Sounds good." Couldn't hurt to stay for a beer, he supposed.

He followed Caleb inside and froze when an all-too-familiar voice reached his ears. Sitting at the kitchen table with a cup of coffee was none other than Miss Stubborn, laughing with Lauren, her head tipped back, looking more beautiful than usual, if that were possible. A ridiculous surge of jealousy seized him by the throat. How come the ornery woman never cracked a smile when he was around?

Carrie looked up and caught sight of him, her smile fading. She shot Caleb a look, then Lauren, who in turn sent Matt a sheepish grin.

A setup? A blind date? He almost laughed, but caught himself. A grin tugged at his lips. The woman looked ready to blow.

"Please tell me he's not the"—Carrie made air quotes—"great guy you've been raving about."

Caleb grabbed a beer from the fridge and handed it to Matt as Carrie glared daggers at her friend. Lauren cleared her throat and looked to Caleb, who shrugged. "We just thought...you know, that you'd hit it off. And we'd planned this before..." Lauren glanced over at Matt.

He took a fortifying sip of his beer and supplied, "Before I opened my big mouth and became her least favorite person in Redemption?"

Carrie scowled at him. "Don't talk about me like I'm not here. And you did more than open your mouth, you pompous ass."

Infuriating woman. Matt took a step forward. "I offered you sound business advice. But, hey, you want to lose your shop? End up in bankruptcy court? Be my guest."

"It's summer!"

"O-kay." Caleb moved to Lauren's side. "Time to calm down. Matt, why don't you have a seat. Carrie, please," Caleb added when she started to rise. "Lauren spent a lot of time and effort making this meal. The least you two can do is sit and eat it."

"You're right," Matt said, embarrassed by his childish behavior. He shot Carrie a look. The woman brought out the worst in him like no one ever had. "Lauren, dinner smells incredible, thank you."

Carrie crossed her arms over her chest and pouted. Matt, hard-pressed not to laugh, took the seat across from her and openly stared. *Let her squirm*, he thought, admiring the view. He took a swig of his beer. The woman was sexy as hell with those big blue eyes and waist-length auburn hair. She wasn't tall and stick thin like Lauren. Carrie had curves...lots and lots of luscious curves. His gaze unwittingly dropped to her chest. He couldn't help it. Matt was a breast man, and Carrie Lowell filled a T-shirt so well it should be a crime.

"Hey, perv, you wanna quit staring at my boobs?"

Matt choked back a laugh. "Kind of hard to do when you put them on display like that."

Her eyes grew round with indignation. "I do not!"

Matt gestured toward her chest. "Well, could that T-shirt be any tighter?"

"Now you're calling me fat?"

Matt thunked his beer down on the table. "Don't put words in my mouth, woman. I was merely—"

"Enough," Caleb broke in. "Jesus, we're going to have to put you both in a time-out if you don't start acting like adults."

"He started it," Carrie pouted, eyes narrowed.

"No, you called me a pompous ass."

"You *are* a pompous ass...perv."

"All right, one more word and you're both getting your mouths duct-taped," Caleb threatened.

"Fine." Matt swiped up his beer and took a long pull.

"*Fine.*"

Supper was eaten mostly in silence. Max and Emma were hanging out with Hutch, owner of the local diner, "so the adults can talk," Caleb informed them. Once Lauren had a slice of cheesecake and a cup of coffee in front of each of them, Caleb got right to the point. "Matt, last week you mentioned you'd like to invest in a business here in Redemption. And Carrie, you were advised to take on a partner if you want to save *Coffee To Chai For*."

Carrie bristled. "Great, announce it to the world, why don't you. Carrie Lowell doesn't have a lick of business sense."

"Come on, Care, that's not what Caleb said." Lauren covered her friend's hand. "But you do need some help, and there's no shame in admitting that."

Carrie shot Matt a quick look. He met her gaze without expression. The woman was a powder keg, and even a twitch of his eye could send her bolting for the door. "Couldn't hurt to talk about it," he said in a low tone.

She pursed her lips and scowled at each of them in turn. "Fine. Start talking."

Chapter Two

Carrie hated feeling beholden to anyone, and she especially hated the thought of letting this arrogant man anywhere near her precious coffee shop. But the alternative was unthinkable. Better to throw in with the devil than lose her business. And truth be told, he'd made some good points, even if she'd let her tongue wither and fall out before admitting it.

Matt leaned back in his chair and met her gaze. Carrie ignored the tingle of awareness those gorgeous eyes caused. "Maybe Caleb and Lauren are on to something. *Coffee To Chai For*'s coffee rivals Starbucks, and your breads and pasties are delicious."

"Go on."

He grinned. "I can offer some fresh business insight, not to mention cash so you can hire someone to help out. You've been running yourself ragged for months. Probably why you're always so crabby."

Her eyes narrowed. "You may have all the business sense of in the world, but you're a moron when it comes to dealing with women."

Lauren snorted. Caleb coughed before shoveling a huge bite of cheesecake into his mouth.

Matt took a sip of his coffee, then forked up a bite of his own cheesecake and took his sweet time chewing and swallowing. Carrie suspected he was holding back a smile, but truthfully, so was she.

"Sorry, bad joke. Just trying to lighten the mood. Seriously, Carrie, I think we'd make a great team. You need a partner, and I need a purpose. I'm afraid being a librarian isn't as exciting and glamorous as you might think. What do you say?"

Carrie cracked a small smile before she could stop herself. Matt's gaze dropped to her lips and she licked them in reflex. *Grrr.* Damn him for making her heart race like a schoolgirl in the throws of puppy love.

"Care, this is exactly what you need," Lauren pointed out, drawing Carrie's attention away from Mr. I'm-Too-Sexy-For-My-Own-Good. "Someone to help shoulder the responsibility. Trying to run the shop all by yourself has been killing you. You're always exhausted and, yes, I'm sorry, but crabbier than usual. You do all your own baking and wait on customers to boot. You need help. And Matt has some pretty good ideas for the place, you have to admit."

Okay, yeah, his suggestions made sense. In fact, Carrie would love to expand her menu to include lunch and dinner items. And if she didn't start each day at three in the morning, she *would* stay open later than two p.m. It's not like she'd never thought of those things herself. She needed help, and she needed it fast. There was just no way around it. If she wanted to keep her business afloat, she'd have to take on a partner.

But did it have to be the one man who'd gotten under her skin like no one ever had? How was she supposed to concentrate on anything when his very presence would drive her to distraction? If she wasn't itching to throttle him, she'd be daydreaming about kissing him. And wouldn't that just suck big time?

"Can you even afford to invest in my shop? I mean, if I'm going to do this, I need someone with the cash in hand, not someone waiting on a loan to go through."

"I've got a decent nest egg saved. But to be clear, I want to be a full partner, not just an investor."

"I know, and that's...fine. Just don't think you're going to come in and take over. *Coffee To Chai For* is my baby."

"I only want to make it the success I know it can be. And make a living for myself so I can eventually quit my job at the library," he added with another heart-melting smile.

Carrie stared at him for a moment before exchanging glances with Lauren and Caleb. After a full minute of silent deliberation, she took a deep breath and blew it out, along with her hesitation. "Fine. Welcome to *Coffee To Chai For*...partner."

Lauren clapped as Matt reached across the table and clasped Carrie's hand. Panic seized her, but she just as quickly tamped it down. Think positive, she silently instructed herself.

"Do you have your own lawyer, or do you trust me to hire one?" Matt asked.

Carrie blew out a hard breath. "I have a lawyer."

Carrie waited until almost ten p.m. before picking up the phone and dialing her lawyer.

"Hello?"

"Hey, it's me. You got a minute?"

"Carrie?"

She rolled her eyes. "It hasn't been that long since we spoke."

"Considering we live just across town from each other, I think a month is a pretty long time. So, what do you need?"

Carrie worried her bottom lip, a stab of guilt nailing her right in the gut. "Maybe I just want to talk to my big sister. Is that so hard to believe?"

"Uh, since the last time we spoke you told me to mind my own business and that the sound of my voice was like nails on a chalkboard, yes, it's that hard to believe."

Carrie couldn't help but grin. "You weren't saying what I wanted to hear. You know how I get when I'm irritated."

"Yeah, mean as a snake," her sister muttered.

Christina Lowell had never been one to mince words. Probably why she was such a great attorney. "So what is it, Care? I don't mean to be rude, but I had a long day and just want to crawl into bed and pass out."

"I decided to take on a partner."

A delicate snort. "Yeah, right."

"I'm serious. His name is Matt Jacobs and—"

"That cute librarian?"

Carrie rolled her eyes, annoyed for some unfathomable reason. "Yes, Tina, the librarian. Figures you've already scoped him out."

"Half the town has, baby sister. That's one mega sexy man. Have you ever seen anyone look so good in a pair of glasses?"

"Can you focus, please?" Carrie plopped down on the couch and leaned her head back. "I need a lawyer to draw up the paperwork. Think you could make time in your busy schedule to do that for me?"

"As if I could refuse such a heartfelt request. I'll be in touch."

Carrie disconnected the call and tossed the phone on the end table. So all the single women in town were panting after Matt. The thought caused her throat to constrict. Old-fashioned jealousy nailed her square between the eyes. And since Christina was successful, gorgeous, and the polar opposite of Carrie, it wouldn't be long before he was panting after her.

A tear seeped out of the corner of her eye and she angrily swiped it away. She didn't give a crap who Matt panted after. Okay, so maybe she did, a little. Maybe a small part of her wondered if this partnership would develop into something more. But, heck, who was she kidding? Men weren't attracted to her, they were scared to death of her, and that's just the way she liked it.

Carrie rolled her eyes when she recognized Matt standing in front of the door to *Coffee To Chai For*, looking entirely too chipper for so early in the morning. The sun hadn't even risen yet, for crump's sake. With a sigh of resignation, she pulled into the parking lot and killed the engine. By the time she grabbed her purse, Matt had her car door open.

"Wow, this thing is spotless." He ran his gaze around the interior of her midnight blue '99 Chevy Malibu. "Wanna clean my Jeep for me?"

She stepped out and lifted a brow. "Uh, no. And what are you doing here so early? I don't open for business until five."

Matt followed her to the door. "Thought I'd give you a hand opening up today, familiarize myself with your routine. The library doesn't open until ten, so I can help you with the baking, the brewing, and the morning rush hour.

Then we can discuss ideas for updating this place and—"

"Oh my God, shut up, will you? You're like the freakin' Energizer Bunny. I like peace and quiet in the morning, not nonstop chatter. Please, please, go home."

Carrie twisted the key in the lock and shoved the door open with more force than necessary. She stormed into the back room and tucked her purse in the bottom drawer of her desk. When she realized Mr. Cheerful had followed her inside, she crossed her arms and turned to face him. "Look, I contacted my lawyer last night, but the paperwork won't be ready for days. So until then, this is still my coffee shop, and I'd like to be alone."

Matt propped his hands on his hips, his expression neutral. "If I promise to keep quiet, can I stay? I'm too hyped up to sleep, and I'll have to learn all this soon enough anyway."

Carrie sucked in a deep breath and let it out slowly. Great. Just what she needed, having to look at his handsome mug all morning. As if she didn't have enough crap to occupy her thoughts. "Fine, whatever. Just keep it zipped, all right?"

"No problem, Sally Sunshine. Show me what to do and I'll stay out of your hair."

She eyeballed him as she swept past. "Know how to work a broom?"

He chuckled. "Not exactly what I had in mind."

"You said you want to learn how to open, right? Well..." She pulled the broom off the wall rack. "I sweep every morning before I unlock the doors."

Later, Carrie had to admit it was nice having Matt there to help out. He worked hard, kept his mouth shut, and even managed to get the air-conditioner running again. For that alone she was incredibly grateful. She just wouldn't tell him that.

Matt was in the back working on her dripping faucet when the bell tinkled and a customer walked in. Carrie recognized the pretty blonde from the day before, the one Tara's brother, Charlie, had asked Carrie to buy a couple of drinks for—on him. "Hi, what can I get you?"

"A large French vanilla cappuccino to go, please."

Carrie made the drink and set it on the counter. When Charlie's blonde pulled money from her pocket, Carrie informed her, "It's already taken care of."

"What? No—"

"Compliments of Charlie Russell." Carrie grinned. "And you still have one more coming."

"Oh." A slight frown marring her brow, she picked up her cup and dropped some money into the tip jar. "Good. Thanks."

"My guess is he's hoping to get your number."

The blonde gave an unladylike snort. "Oh, I've already got his, and guess what? It's not going to happen."

Carrie chuckled as the woman strolled out the door. Charlie had no doubt met his match with that one.

Whistling, Matt strode through the swinging door that separated the kitchen from the dining area and headed straight for the counter. He seemed rather pleased with himself. "All fixed. Anything else I can do before I head over to the library?"

"No, thanks. I owe you for the air-conditioner. I have to admit, Jacobs, I'm impressed. You're a hard worker, and that's something I value."

His brow rose. "I'm sorry, did you just compliment me?"

She pursed her lips in an effort to hold back a grin, but lost the battle. "Don't get used to it." Her pulse sped up when he reached out and traced her jaw line with his fingertips, his gaze centered on her lips.

"Do you have any idea how beautiful you are?"

Carrie suddenly became lost in those gorgeous eyes and that handsome face. Words failed her. She swallowed hard and fought to keep from melting at his feet. He started to lean in and Carrie panicked. Did he mean to kiss her? Right here in the shop where anyone could see them?

The door opened with a tinkling sound and Matt snatched his hand back, looking like a guilty little boy. Talk about saved by the bell. Carrie cleared her throat and smiled as a couple of teenaged girls walked up to the counter. Her smiled faded when she realized they weren't there as customers. They both gazed up at Matt, their heavily made-up faces pathetically adoring.

"Hi," the curly-haired blonde cooed as her brunette friend clutched onto her arm, looking about ready to faint. Carrie rolled her eyes.

Matt met her gaze, amusement dancing in his eyes, before shooting the girls a wink. "What can I get for you ladies?"

"We were just wondering...what time does the library open?"

"In about two minutes. Come on, I'll walk you over."

He glanced at Carrie. "Same time tomorrow?"

"I'll be counting the minutes," she muttered.

Chapter Three

"A limited liability partnership?" Carrie echoed as she held her back screen door open and waved her sister in.

Tina took a seat at Carrie's kitchen table, opened her briefcase, and pulled out a thin stack of papers. Her sharp blue gaze quickly moved over the papers in her hand. As always, she looked professional yet stylish, not to mention beautiful. Her espresso-brown plain weave pantsuit—no doubt Anne Klein—fit her slim frame to perfection, a cream silk scarf draped around her throat, and matching pointy-toe pumps peeked out from beneath her flared slacks. A gold clip held her long, dark brown waves up in a loose twist.

"Yes. Limited liability means a person's financial liability is limited to a fixed sum, usually the value of a person's investment. A shareholder in a limited liability company isn't personally liable for any of the company's debts other than the value of their investment.

"Limited liability partnerships are run like general partnerships and have a similar degree of management flexibility. Income, losses, and gains are passed through to the general partners according to the partnership agreement.

"If there is no partnership agreement, income, losses, and gains will be allocated in proportion to the partnership interests of each partner. Partners can agree among themselves as to how income, losses, and gains are divided among the partners. The partners then report the amount allocated on their own income tax returns and pay tax accordingly."

Carrie sighed. "Layman terms, please."

Tina chuckled. "Trust me, this is the best way for both of you. Especially since you're in desperate need of cash. A full partnership takes a long time to establish, and you need the help—not to mention the cash—right away. I can literally get the paperwork rolling tomorrow."

Although she certainly was in desperate need of cash, it somehow stung more hearing her sister say it. Carrie had always been sort of the black sheep of the family as far as careers were concerned. Both of her parents were prominent attorneys, as was their darling older daughter. Carrie's big brother was a cop, and her baby brother a graphic designer.

"If you're sure. I'll have Matt meet us at the shop around...?"

"You know, it's only seven thirty. Why don't you give him a call and see if he can stop by now. You two can get the papers signed tonight."

Carrie's heart flipped in her chest. "Please tell me this isn't about you wanting to flirt with him."

"I could flirt with him in the morning, if that were my intention," Tina pointed out, rising to her feet. "And I'd be fresh and perky instead of tired and cranky. Go on, give him a call while I put on a pot of coffee. Got any plain ol' Maxwell House?"

Carrie pulled into the parking lot of *Coffee To Chai For* and let out a whopper of a sigh when she saw who stood at the front of the shop, waiting for her. Wasn't it enough she'd dreamt about the man all night long, tossing and turning, getting very little sleep?

He strode over and opened her car door. Carrie knew it was ridiculous to get angry over his gentlemanly behavior, but that didn't stop her jaw from clenching when he reached for her hand.

"Thanks, but I'm perfectly capable of getting out of my car all by myself."

"Sorry, forgot you're not a morning person." He stepped back and stuck his hands in his pockets.

Great, now she felt like a class A witch. She grabbed her purse and climbed out. "No, I'm sorry. I, uh, didn't sleep very well."

"Forget it."

"I'm just not used to having to talk so early in the morning." She opened the door and flipped on the lights.

Matt chuckled. "I swear I've never met another woman like you."

She cast him a quick glance over her shoulder as she headed into the back room. "Sounds like a cleverly veiled insult to me."

"I don't know about clever since you figured it right out."

She rolled her eyes. "I guess I'll teach you how to use all the equipment today. The espresso machine can be especially ornery, so we'll start with that."

"Sounds like a plan."

By the time nine o'clock rolled around, Carrie was ready to drop-kick Matt across the street to the library.

"Why are you being so stubborn about this?" he demanded as he followed her around like a drill sergeant. "I thought you understood that in order to save this place you'd have to make certain changes."

"The only change I want to make is who I took on as a partner last night," she groused. Matt had come right over the night before and listened as Tina explained about the limited liability partnership. He'd even agreed that it made the most sense. They'd had a cup of coffee, and she'd ushered him out the door the first time Tina batted her eyelashes at him. Okay, so maybe she'd overreacted, but frankly she hadn't been in the mood to watch Matt fawn all over her perfect sister.

The bell jangled and Carrie looked up in time to watch Charlie's blonde goddess walk through the door, Charlie hot on her heels. Carrie gave a silent chuckle. *'Not going to happen,' huh, Blondie?*

Both were dressed in shorts and sweating, as if they'd just finished a major work out.

Figured, the woman was a fitness buff on top of being gorgeous and funny. Just like Tina. Carrie glanced down at her overabundance of curves and cringed.

Charlie joined them at the counter. "Morning, Carrie. Matt," he said with a curious glance at her new partner.

"Morning, Charlie." She eyed Blondie again, wondering if Charlie would make the introductions.

"This is Dana McClain, Allie's cousin," Charlie supplied, as if reading her mind.

"Nice to officially meet you," Dana said, a smile tugging at her lips.

Her smile was genuine; Carrie liked her, despite the fact she was disgustingly perfect. Maybe she was even good enough for Charlie, one of the very few decent guys left in the world.

Carrie chanced a quick glance over at Matt, expecting a foot-long string of drool to be hanging from his mouth. Oddly enough, he was glaring daggers at Charlie.

Now what the heck could Charlie have done to warrant such a look?

"Yeah, you, too. Nice to put a name to the face. This is Matt Jacobs, my new partner."

Charlie frowned. "New partner? No shit?"

"No shit," Matt confirmed, crossing his arms over his chest, his tone borderline hostile. Carrie exchanged looks with Dana, who seemed to be enjoying the surge of testosterone.

"We signed the papers last night," Carrie admitted. She knew exactly what Charlie was thinking—that hell had frozen over. "So, what can we get for you?"

Dana looked up and studied the menu. "I think I'll have...a Chai tea today. Large, please."

"And I'll have my usual," Charlie said, casting Matt one last curious look.

Carrie turned to Matt. "Would you like to make the Chai tea?"

"Since I have no friggin' idea what Charlie's 'usual' is, what else would I make?"

Once Matt turned around to brew the tea, Carrie met Charlie's amused gaze with an apologetic 'I-have-no-idea-what-his-problem-is' shrug before making his usual French roast with two sugars and one cream. Charlie winked at her as she slid his cup across the counter. Matt plunked Dana's tea down beside it, steam practically blowing from his ears. He'd seen the wink...though why that should bother him was beyond her.

Charlie paid for their drinks, settling his tab in the process. Carrie had hoped they'd leave;

she didn't want any witnesses when she tore Matt's arm off and used it to club him to death. But Charlie, the devil, escorted Dana over to one of tables.

Carrie spun around and glowered at Matt, mystified by his Jekyll and Hyde behavior. "What the hell is your problem? Charlie is one of my dearest friends, and if you think I'm gonna let you take it out on him because you're mad at me, you can think again."

Matt leaned forward and braced one hand on the wall behind her, his stormy gaze intense. Carrie's breath caught. Lord, the man was sexy. Feelings long buried broke to the surface and every nerve in her body sizzled to life.

"Are you in love with him?"

Her eyes widened. She had to swallow down a bubble of hysterical laughter. "With Charlie? Have you lost your mind? That's what all this macho crap was about?"

"I don't hear you denying it." He shot a quick look over to where Dana and Charlie were pretending not to listen in. Thank God Matt had been wise enough to speak in a low tone. Although she couldn't be sure, it was a pretty safe bet Charlie would wipe the floor with him.

"I don't have to defend myself to you, and it's none of your damn business who I date. But for the record, Charlie is a friend, nothing more." She tried to shove him away from her, but the infuriating man didn't budge. He was built a little more solidly than she'd thought. Resisting the urge to run her hands over his muscled chest, she propped them on her hips. "Ever hear the expression 'personal space'?" she snapped.

"Ever hear the expression 'put you over my knee'?"

She chanced a glance at Charlie and Dana, who both quickly looked away. And was Charlie...grinning? Traitorous idiot. "You put one hand on me and I'll have you thrown in jail so fast it'll make your head spin! My brother happens to be a cop."

Her raised voice seemed to do the trick. Matt muttered a curse and stepped back, swiping his fingers through his hair. "Look, I'm sorry. I had no right to go off on you like that. Blame it on stress...hell, I don't know, blame it on the fact I'm crazy about—"

"Oh, my God, did you see that?" Carrie couldn't believe her eyes. Dana dumped her tea right in Charlie's lap, then shot up and walked out of the shop with her head held high, like some regal queen. Charlie chased after her without so much as a glance in Carrie's direction. Carrie had no idea what Charlie said to provoke Dana, but she had no doubt he deserved it. Friend or not, Charlie Russell was a man, and all men were idiots.

She turned back to Matt. "Well, I have a mess to mop up, and you need to go open the library. Besides, I think the two of us have said enough for one day."

Matt stared at her for a tension-charged moment, then turned and strode out the door. Carrie watched him cross the street as his heat-filled question replayed in her mind. "Are you in love with him?"

If she didn't know better, she'd swear the guy was jealous. But that was impossible. Men weren't attracted to full-figured women like her—at least not for anything serious. They went for the supermodel types like her neighbor Lauren, or her sister Tina, or Dana. Carrie had learned that the hard way three years ago.

"I guess you should congratulate me," Matt muttered when Caleb walked into the library a couple hours later. "We signed the papers last night. Did you know her sister's an attorney?"

Caleb set his books down on the return pile and picked up one of the magazines Matt had just unpacked. "Yeah, Lauren mentioned it. Both her parents are as well. So congrats, man...I think. You don't sound all that thrilled."

"Let's just say I stuck my foot in my mouth earlier. Had a little visit from the green-eyed monster and acted like a jerk. I don't suppose you know Charlie Russell?"

Caleb chuckled. "As a matter of fact, I walked up just as Charlie was asking Lauren out last month at the fair. Yep, took me a while to warm up to ol' Charlie. Why? I know he and Carrie are friends, but—"

"They're just friends, you're sure?" Matt knew he must sound like a fool, but jealousy was a new emotion for him, and obviously he didn't deal with it very well.

"I'm sure, man, settle down. They've known each other since like high school, maybe before."

Matt gave a curt nod, not completely convinced. Christ, he had it bad. He couldn't even remember the last time he'd been this gut-twisted over a woman. Maybe never.

"So, is this partnership a done deal, or will it be a while before it's legal?"

Matt explained about the limited liability partnership, which his own attorney had suggested as well. "I gave my two-week notice this morning. Felt good, I have to admit. I wasn't meant to work in a library."

Caleb tossed the magazine down and grinned. "Are you kidding? This place has become a regular hotspot since you started." He flicked his chin toward the tables, which were filled with women of all ages, many of them blatantly staring at Matt instead of their books.

Mrs. Langhart, Matt realized with a soft chuckle, had her book held upside down. He gestured for her to flip it right-side up. She sent him a sheepish grin and gave her silver bob a quick pat before righting the calculus textbook.

Caleb gave him a thump on the back. "If that woman knows the difference between a product rule and a quotient rule, I'll eat my boot. See you later, stud."

"Smartass."

Matt waited until Mary showed up before taking his lunch break. Normally, he packed a cold lunch and ate it in the back room, but today he had a taste for something hot. And since he owed a certain gorgeous brunette a huge apology, he might as well start by buying her lunch. In fact—he glanced at his cell phone—she should be closing up shop right about now. He stuffed his hands in his pockets, blew out a here-goes-nothing breath, and made his way across the street.

He arrived just as Carrie was locking up. "Hey, partner, care to join me for lunch? My treat." She looked as beautiful as ever with the sun reflecting off the auburn highlights in her hair and those huge enigmatic blue eyes gazing up at him with uncertainty.

She let out an exaggerated breath. He was no doubt the last person with whom she cared to share a meal, and with good reason. He'd really made an ass of himself earlier.

"Come on, the least you can do is give me a chance to apologize for acting like a five-year-old this morning. We can just talk business...or not at all, if you prefer. Your choice."

"Fine. I'm not in the mood to cook anyway. Where are you taking me?"

"Nino's. I've had a taste for one of their Italian beef sandwiches all day. Sound good?"

"Sounds great. Their antipasto salad is my favorite.

"Hop in, I'll drive."

The atmosphere inside Nino's put Matt right at ease, with its checkered tablecloths and old-world ambiance. Reminded him of his favorite Italian restaurant in New York City's West Village. And much to his delight, the food was even better.

One of Nino's sons showed them to a booth in the corner. "How're you two doin' today? Either of you need a menu?"

"Thanks, but I think we both know what we want." Matt gestured for Carrie to order first.

"I'll have a side antipasto salad, a cup of minestrone, and an iced tea, please."

When he finished writing, Matt said, "I'll have an Italian beef sandwich, dipped, with sweet peppers, and a side of fried zucchini with extra ranch dressing. Oh, and a large Pepsi."

The kid nodded. "I'll be right back with your drinks."

"So," Matt said, drawing her attention back to him. "I turned in my resignation at the library today. Two more weeks and I'm all yours."

"I can hardly contain my excitement."

Matt grinned. "You're hell on a man's ego, you know that?"

"In case you haven't noticed, you and I get along about as well as Wile E. Coyote and the Roadrunner." She glanced away and tucked a stray lock of hair behind her ear. "Besides, with every woman in town between the ages of sixteen and sixty panting after you, I'm sure your ego will survive my indifference."

Hmm, did he sense a little jealousy there, or was it simply wishful thinking on his part? "You looked anything but indifferent yesterday when you thought I was going to kiss you."

"Do me a favor and get over yourself before we start to work together full-time. *Coffee To Chai For* is too small to fit you, me, and your inflated head."

He chuckled. "Good one. And you're right. With your bad attitude taking up most of the back room, we're pretty cramped for space."

Carrie rolled her eyes and shook her head, but she couldn't quite hide the smile tugging at her lips. She plucked a bunch of sugar packets out of the tray a second before their drinks were set on the table. Matt watched with interest as she stirred the sugar into her iced tea, then gave the lemon wedge a squeeze before dropping it back in her glass. She licked the tart juice from her fingers, one after the other, almost as if in slow motion. He swallowed a groan, thankful to be seated. She cast him a quick glance, one finger still in her mouth, which was so damn sexy it had to have been perfected in the mirror.

He cleared his throat. "Maybe we could talk about some of my ideas, if you don't mind."

Her expression became guarded again, and
Matt could've kicked himself. But there was no
help for it. If this partnership was going to
work, then little Miss Stubborn was going to
have to give a little. Or a lot.

"Fine, talk."

"I think the two most important things we'll
need to focus on are extending the hours and
adding a lunch-slash-dinner menu. Since this
town already has a fantastic diner and the best
Italian food in the state, I think a more health-
conscious menu would be a hit. Wraps and
sandwiches, soups and salads. Juice blends, fruit
smoothies, maybe a selection of bottled waters."

Carrie took a thoughtful sip of her tea. "To
be honest, I've wanted to expand the menu for
some time. But without money to hire a couple
of full-time employees, not to mention all the
food and supplies I'd need, I knew it was just a
pipedream." She lowered her gaze. "As you
well know, I've barely been able to keep the
doors open."

He reached across the table and grasped her
hand. "You'll never have to worry about that
again, I promise you. I plan to make sure *Coffee
To Chai For* becomes a thriving success. And
without you having to work your fingers to the
bone seven days a week."

Her expression grew defensive. "I don't mind hard work. It builds character."

"Sweetheart, you have more character than anyone I know," he teased, wondering if it'd been her parents who'd drummed that into her head. "Come on, admit it. Wouldn't it be nice to be able to sleep in once in a while? To not have to worry about who's going to make the coffee or do the baking?"

She gave a reluctant nod. "I'd be lying if I said no. But let's face it, that day is still a long way off."

"Turn up the volume!" someone shouted before Matt could respond. His gaze was drawn to the TV mounted above the bar. Looked like some sort of news conference was about to start. He was momentarily distracted when Carrie slipped her hand from his.

"As reported this morning, Jacob Spalding Sr., CEO of Spalding Industries, the largest family-owned business in the United States, was admitted into Cedars-Sinai Hospital late Sunday evening with severe chest pains. His family released this short statement today: 'Mr. Spalding is getting the best care possible and is expected to make a full recovery.'

"The Spalding family made headlines early last fall when son and future CEO, Jacob

Spalding Jr., who hasn't been seen publicly in over six months, was arrested in connection with the murder of actress Amanda Ames. He was cleared of all charges after a DNA test proved him innocent. In local news..."

Matt continued to stare at the TV even though he didn't hear another word the anchorman said. Shock warred with concern for his father—concern won. He pulled his cell phone from his shirt pocket and pushed his chair back. "I just remembered something I need to tell Mary. I'll be right back."

Chapter Four

Carrie watched Matt leave with mixed feelings. Maybe taking him on as her partner wasn't as smart a move as she'd thought. When the man wasn't insulting her friends and acting the fool, he was running outside to make secretive calls. Really, what top-secret library news couldn't be talked about in front of her? Nino's didn't have a "no cell phone" policy.

Another problem was her growing attraction to him. Matt Jacobs was the first man to make her feel anything since the day she'd kicked her ex out of the house. Not that she'd intended to live celibate forever. It's just sex without love wasn't a choice she'd have made—until now. Damn his sexy hide, Matt had her thinking all sorts of naughty thoughts, which only fueled her annoyance.

The restaurant door opened, and Matt walked back in. He returned to the table and greeted her with a smile that didn't quite reach his eyes. Matt Jacobs, man of mystery. Oh, well, everyone had a few secrets, right? And really, unless whatever he was hiding interfered with her business, his personal life was certainly none of hers.

She'd just had to remind herself of that daily.

"Sorry about that. Mary's doing inventory tonight, and I forgot to tell her where I'd left off."

He was lying through his teeth, no doubt about it. Carrie forced a smile. "No problem. And you're just in time, here comes the food."

They ate in silence until the waiter arrived with dessert—Nino's famous chocolate chip cannolis. Unbidden, a mental image of all the gorgeous skinny women in her life popped into her mind, and her confidence plummeted. She pushed the dessert plate away.

"Please tell me you didn't forget to save room for a cannoli."

"No. I'm just full. Would you like mine?"

He held up a hand as if warding off evil. "Sorry, one's my limit. I have to watch this girlish figure." He grinned, and although Carrie knew he was teasing, and knew he couldn't possibly know how insecure she was about her weight, she grabbed her purse and rose to her feet.

Matt tossed his napkin down and also stood. A frown marred his handsome face. "Did I say something wrong? Because if I did, I'm sorry. Seems that's all do when I'm around you, put my foot in my mouth and apologize."

"No, I just…I need to get home. Thanks for the late lunch. So, will I be seeing you again tomorrow morning?" It killed her to admit it, even in the privacy of her own mind, but she certainly hoped so.

He shot her a wink. "Bright-eyed and bushy-tailed, just the way you like me."

A smile tugged at her lips. "Need a ride back to the library?"

"Nah, I'm going to enjoy my cannoli. Yours too, unless you want to bring it home?"

"Thanks, but it's all yours. Enjoy."

"That I will. See you in the morning, boss. Oh, and I meant to ask, could I get a key for the coffee shop?"

Carrie stared at him, not sure what to say. He was her partner. He'd need a key eventually. She just wasn't quite ready to let go of the last thing that made *Coffee To Chai For* hers and hers alone. "I...yeah, sure. Just remind me later."

By Friday afternoon, Carrie realized she was dangerously close to falling in love with Matt Jacobs. The admission came not so much as a shock as an epiphany. He was funny, smart, charming, wickedly handsome, and sexy as hell. Carrie wanted him more than she'd ever wanted anyone or anything in her life. He had her so twisted in knots, she hadn't gotten a good night's sleep since the day they'd signed the papers.

He showed up every morning to help her open, learning in record time how to run the machines, bake the breads, pastries and cookies she'd become famous for. He'd managed to fix the air-conditioner, so that was one less thing they'd need to invest in. At least until next summer. He'd gotten an affordable bid on the construction for the dining area to accommodate the extra tables and booths they'd need for the new lunch/dinner menu in the works, and also on adding a drive-thru window, though Carrie wasn't completely sold on the latter idea. Something they'd have to hold off on until she felt more comfortable with the thought of so many changes. Especially since her business, in just these few days, had started to thrive.

Okay, so many of her newest customers were adoring females. But since Matt seemed to only have eyes for her, even her insecurities had abated. He'd yet to try and kiss her, but Carrie figured he was just waiting for her cue.

Tonight she planned to give it to him. Yeah, she was a long way off from trusting her heart to another man. Love and trust didn't necessarily go hand in hand; she'd learned that the hard way. Didn't mean she couldn't see where things led with Matt.

She'd just hung the Now Hiring sign in the shop's front window when the screech of tires caught her attention. She looked up just in time to see an expensive-looking red sports car fishtail down Salvation Avenue and squeal to a stop in front of the Laundromat next door. Immediately, she saw the reason the car had spun out of control. Standing on the other side of the street was Drew Porter, owner of D.P. Tire & Auto, holding the collar of his humongous Great Dane, Bo, wrestling to keep him in check.

Since the shop was empty at the moment, Carrie grabbed her cell phone and raced outside to make sure the driver was all right. The car door swung open just as Carrie reached it, and out came one high-heeled black pump, followed by another. Carrie rolled her eyes as an incredibly beautiful supermodel type stepped out of the car and glanced around, her perfectly manicured hands on her hips. She had long, platinum blond hair, big brown eyes, and a pair of sunglasses propped stylishly on her head. Her skintight little black dress ended just above her knees. Surprisingly, she didn't have on a single accessory, but then, she didn't need any.

The woman's eyes narrowed when she spotted Drew and Bo on the other side of the street. She started toward them, and Bo bounced excitedly on his hindquarters, tongue lolling, tail thumping the grass.

Carrie couldn't hold back a smile when she recognized the resigned look on Drew's face.

"Are you crazy letting that beast roam free? Doesn't Mayberry here have a leash law?"

A wolfish grin transformed Drew's face as he eyed the woman from head to toe. Typical, Carrie thought, resisting the urge to throw a rock across the street and knock some sense into him. "Look, I'm sorry. Bo doesn't usually take off like that. Must've seen a cat or something. If you have any damages just drive down the road to D.P. Tire & Auto and I'll take care of 'em."

"Damn right you will," she declared with a toss of her head, striking a pose.

Great, Carrie thought with another eye roll. Just what Redemption needed, Paris Hilton's long-lost twin.

"Lindy?"

Carrie glanced up when she heard Matt's voice. She watched with growing dismay as he strode across the street, not toward her, but straight for the blonde.

"Matt!" the woman cried as she spun around and ran up to meet him—no easy feat in those heels. She launched herself into Matt's arms, and the louse caught her in a crushing embrace.

Devastated, Carrie's face burned with humiliation as she watched the scene before her. Matt pulled back and grinned down at the gorgeous twit—he'd certainly never looked at her like that.

With a heavy heart, Carrie turned away and headed back into the shop. She had no desire to watch Matt fawn all over another woman. God, what a fool she'd been. She'd actually started to believe there was something between them, that he was as crazy for her as she was him. What a joke. Men didn't want a woman with a little extra meat on her bones. They wanted the skinny supermodel types. Men...maybe she should just switch teams and become a lesbian.

"What are you doing here, Lindy?" Matt stepped back and scowled at his impulsive baby sister. "I told you not to come. I can't afford to have the paparazzi swoop in and screw everything up."

"Settle down, I was careful. Besides, I don't plan to stay long. Just until you've had a chance to pack your bags. I'm taking you home." Lindy glanced around, her disdain for the small Midwest town clear. "You don't belong here anymore than I do."

Before Matt could respond, Drew strode up, a firm grip on Bo's collar. He was dressed in his navy blue mechanic's uniform, his gaze for Lindy and Lindy alone. Matt had to swallow a chuckle. Maybe his sister would discover a reason to stay in Redemption after all.

Lindy pulled her sunglasses down on her nose and turned to face him. "Is there something I can do for you?"

Drew grinned and gave her an insulting once-over. "I can think of lots of things, Hot

Stuff, but I'm too much of a gentleman to say them out loud."

"My God, you're rude," she huffed, sticking out a hip. "Matt could be my fiancé for all you know."

Drew gave his head a confident shake. "Not a chance. Anyone with two brain cells can see he only has eyes for Carrie."

"Then how did you figure it out?"

Drew's smile faded. "Careful, Hot Stuff, I may have been lying about the gentleman part."

Matt gave Drew a pat on the back. "Easy, man, that's my baby sister you're talking to."

Drew gave a curt nod. "Sorry, Matt. Didn't mean any disrespect."

"Forget it. Now, would one of you like to tell me what happened? I heard tires screeching, but that's it."

"This horse ran in front of my car and forced me off the road." She pointed an accusing, red-enameled nail at Bo, who started to shimmy and whine with excitement. "It's a miracle I didn't lose control and crash." Lindy put on her "pout face", the one she'd perfected to bring men to their knees. Men she was interested in, that is. And while Drew Porter had a bit of a wild reputation, Caleb seemed to think pretty highly of him, and that held a lot of weight with Matt.

Besides, Lindy was twenty-five years old and plenty capable of taking care of herself.

"Look, I said I was sorry. Let's go take a look and see if you have any damage."

"If there's even so much as a scratch, I want it fixed. This car isn't even three months old."

Drew dragged Bo over to Lindy's car, muttering something under his breath about spoiled blonde brats. Well, Matt couldn't argue with him there. While there was much more to Lindy than met the eye, baby sister sure did enjoy the finer things in life. The fact she was even toying with a small-town, blue-collar guy would make front page news in L.A.

"See? Not a scratch. You kicked up a little dust is all. If you want your car washed, bring it by. I have a drive-thru car wash on the lot."

Lindy's eyes widened in comical dismay. "You're joking, right? This is a Ferrari, Lou."

"Drew."

"You don't run a Ferrari through an automatic car wash."

Drew stared at Lindy for a moment, no doubt trying to decide if she was joking or not. "Whatever. Listen, I have a business to get back to. Have a nice life, Hot Stuff. If you change your mind about the car wash, Matt knows where to find me."

Once Drew was out of earshot, Lindy snarked, "I can see why you're so drawn to this place. The locals are quite charming."

Matt gave his head an exasperated shake. "You know I'm trying to keep a low profile, yet you drive a two-hundred-thousand dollar sports car into town. What the hell were you thinking? And don't bother with the pout, Lindy."

She crossed her arms defensively. "I was thinking that I missed my big brother who I haven't seen in months."

He gazed at her, feeling her pain and uncertainty. They'd always been close, so when he'd decided to drop out of sight and go into hiding, she'd taken it pretty hard. And truthfully, he'd never intended to stay away forever. He'd just needed some time to heal after everything that had happened. Time without paparazzi cameras constantly flashing in his face. "I know, and I'm sorry. But as crazy as it may sound, this place has become my home. I feel alive here in a way I never did in L.A."

She tried to joke his declaration away. "Must have something to do with this Carrie person. Maybe it's time I met her."

"Christ, I forgot about Carrie. Lord only knows what her mind cooked up over you throwing yourself into my arms." He took off for the coffee shop.

Carrie was in the process of refilling the sugar shakers when he and Lindy walked in, Lindy clinging possessively to his arm. Mr. Krawczyk, who worked at the Laundromat, gave him a quick nod on his way out, coffee in hand. Carrie flicked him a glance, her gaze moving down to where Lindy clung to his arm before dismissing them both.

Matt heaved a sigh and strode up to the counter.

"Can you look at me, please?"

"I know what you look like."

"Yep," Lindy drawled as she let go of Matt's arm. "Charming. I totally get why you love this place."

"Lindy, shush. Carrie, I'd like you to meet my sister, Melinda...Jacobs. Lindy, Carrie Lowell, my friend and business partner."

"Sister?" Carrie said, eyeing Lindy warily. "You didn't mention your sister was coming to town."

"That's because I didn't know she was coming." He shot Lindy an accusatory look.

"Oh."

Matt grinned. "Oh? That's it?"

Carrie crossed her arms, her expression somewhat sheepish. "Well, how was I supposed to know? Some rich, beautiful woman arrives in town and..." Her brow creased as she looked from Lindy back to him. "Are you guys rich or something?"

Matt wanted to drop-kick Lindy back to L.A. Couldn't she have at least driven an inconspicuous car rental into town? Damn it, he wasn't ready for this yet. He could lose Carrie if she found out the truth—when she found out the truth—which was inevitable, he knew. But he'd hoped to have more time for Carrie to develop feelings for him so that she didn't bolt when she learned his true identity.

"No," Lindy replied, drumming her nails on the counter. "That's my boss's car. He has a thing for me." She shrugged, as if that said it all, then glanced up at the menu. "So, how are the iced cappuccinos in this place?"

"The best in Redemption," Carrie proudly declared.

"Who's your competition? Dairy Queen?"

"Lindy," Matt warned in a low tone.

Much to his surprise, Carrie chuckled. "Don't worry about it. I have a sister, too." She made Lindy's drink, and then set it on the counter with a self-satisfied grin. "Lindy, prepare to eat your words."

Lindy met her gaze in silent challenge as she picked it up, stuffed in a straw, and took a sip.

She made a classic "not bad" face and took a few more sips. "Definitely better than Dairy Queen."

"The 'Queen' of all compliments," Carrie replied with a roll of her eyes. "Thanks."

Returning her attention to Matt, Carrie crooked her neck and looked up at him with those big blue eyes, a mysterious twinkle hidden in their depths. It took quite a bit of effort not to leap across the counter and carry her off to the back room. She excited him like no other woman ever had. It amazed him that they'd yet to even share a kiss.

"I was wondering," she said in a low tone. "How would you like to come to my place for supper tonight?"

Before Matt could open his mouth, Lindy said, "May I assume I'm included in the invitation? I mean, you don't expect me to sit alone in some motel room on my first night in town, do you?"

"Of course not. The invitation was meant for both of you. I'm making cream of potato soup, ham soufflé, and fried zucchini." She smiled up at him. "I bought an extra-large bottle of ranch dressing."

"Hidden Valley?" Jesus, the woman could make a bottle of salad dressing sound sexy.

"Yep. Only the best for my company."

Lindy hooked her arm through his, and Matt didn't need to look to imagine her pained expression. "Okay, well, I'm about five seconds away from going into sugar shock, so can you two continue this love fest later? I'd like to take a hot bath and wash my hair."

Matt gave an apologetic shake of his head. "Sorry. Lindy's just crabby because Drew Porter didn't melt at her feet."

"I am not!" Lindy hotly denied. "What would I want with that grease monkey?"

"Careful," Carrie warned. "Drew's a friend. He's a hard worker and a good guy, too, so maybe you shouldn't judge people by what they do for a living."

"Whatever. Matt, I'll be outside."

He blew out an exasperated breath. "Again, sorry. I swear, she's not—"

"Usually like that?" Carrie finished for him, waving off Lindy's bad behavior. "Don't worry about it. She obviously adores you, so a certain amount of resentment toward anyone she feels has kept you away is probably normal."

He grinned. "How understanding of you."

"Tell anybody and I'll deny it."

As soon as he stepped outside, Lindy rolled her eyes at him.

"Well, the mystery is solved. Angelina Jolie eyes and Dolly Parton boobs. Matt, you're so predictable."

Chapter Five

Matt pulled into the driveway of his cottage and killed the engine. Lindy pulled the Ferrari up next to his Jeep and stepped out, following him up to the door. He waited until she'd had a chance to freshen up before asking the question he'd wanted to ask since the moment he raced out of the library and recognized her. "How's Dad."

"Took you long enough to ask."

He opened the fridge and grabbed a can of soda. "Can you please not give me a hard time about this? I feel guilty enough without you adding to it."

She seemed genuinely surprised by his admission. "Why would you feel guilty? Dad had a heart attack. How is that your fault?"

"Lindy..."

"He's fine, Matt. Crabby that his days of bacon and Yum Yum Donuts are over, but if he changes his diet and makes use of the exercise room once in a while, he'll be good as new in no time."

"Thank God. And Mom?"

"Matt, why don't you just give her a call? I mean, this is ridiculous. Mom asking me how you are, you asking me how mom is, both of you acting like it's no big deal that you haven't spoken in almost a year."

Matt guzzled half his soda, hoping the lump in his throat would go down with it. "I have called," he admitted, meeting her stunned gaze. "Several times. But she plays the phone tag game, not answering her cell, leaving messages on my home phone when she knows I'm at the library."

"I had no idea. She asks about you constantly: how is he, do I think he'll ever come home, etcetera. I just assumed...She's never told me you've actually tried to call her. And you've never mentioned it either."

Matt shrugged, not sure what to say. Truthfully, stubborn pride was the reason he'd never mentioned it, and no doubt the reason his mother hadn't either. They were two peas in a pod, both as stubborn as the day was long. "Listen, I've got some work to do on the computer. Can you amuse yourself for a couple hours?"

"End of discussion, I get it." She stood up and started searching through his cabinets. "Got any munchies?"

Matt nearly choked on his tongue when Carrie answered the door. The woman was beautiful, no doubt about it, but she rarely wore makeup, or jewelry, or flattering clothes—although the way she filled out a simple, baby-doll T-shirt, it was a miracle she hadn't yet caused a riot.

Tonight she wore a skintight pair of boot-cut, stonewashed jeans and a sexy black tube blouse with a corset-type neckline that clung to her breasts and flared out over her hips. Big sexy gold hoops hung from her ears, her gorgeous shiny auburn hair hung down to her waist—

Matt loved long hair on a woman. To him, nothing was sexier. She wore shiny lip gloss that would have already needed reapplying if Lindy wasn't standing beside him. But what really took his breath away were her eyes. Dark and sultry and heavy on the eyeliner. Maybe Lindy would fall into a food coma after supper so he and Carrie could finally have some alone time.

"You look beautiful." Damn, did that sound lame? "I mean, you always look beautiful, but that blouse...wow." Great, he'd turned into a babbling idiot who couldn't quit looking at her boobs. He used every bit of self-control he had to keep his eyes from wandering down to her chest, but it was hard. Until Lindy gave him an elbow in the side.

"So, is dinner ready? I'm starving."

Carrie smiled and gestured for them to enter. "Just about. I have the deep fryer on; I'll fry the zucchini while we eat since they cook fast and taste so much better fresh out of the oil."

"Amazing your skin is as clear as it is."

Carrie shot Lindy a look, but didn't bother with a reply. For that, Matt was grateful.

They followed Carrie through the house, and Matt glanced around, impressed with the simplicity of her décor. Her living room was done in earth tones; a dark beige couch and matching armchair, a coffee table with a few magazines neatly spread across the top, a gold-framed mirror over the couch. Several photos—of family, he assumed, since he recognized her sister Tina—covered the wall behind the chair.

Her kitchen appliances were white and stainless steel, just like Matt's apartment back in L.A. Carrie motioned for them to sit, then served the cream of potato soup, which looked and smelled incredible. It hadn't dawned on Matt that Carrie would be a good cook, and he felt like a schmuck for not giving her more credit. Especially since she was famous around town for her pastries.

Lindy dipped her spoon in and took a dainty taste. Her brow lifted. "This is pretty good. I'm not usually big on cream soups, but I'm almost tempted to ask for the recipe."

"I'm glad you like it. And I'd be happy to share the recipe, just let me know. Okay, first batch of fried zucchini's done." She scooped the golden brown slices out of the deep fryer, deposited them onto a paper-towel-lined plate, and sprinkled them with a little kosher salt.

Matt grabbed one as soon as he could pick it up without burning his fingers. After a quick dunking in the ranch dressing, he took a cautious bite. "Mmm!" He looked at the breading. "I don't know your secret, but these are even better than Nino's. And if you tell him I said that, I'll deny it."

Carrie winked at him and his heart sped up. "Your secret's safe with me."

Lindy reached for a piece of the zucchini and took a small bite. Her eyes widened and she nodded her approval, popping the rest into her mouth with a thumbs up. Carrie served the ham soufflé next, which was equally amazing, and Lindy ended up asking for recipes for everything. Carrie, not quite as surprised as Matt seemed to be, happily forked them over, even the one for the chocolate mocha trifle she served for dessert.

"Wow," Lindy said as she scraped up the last spoonful of trifle. "I think I must've gained ten pounds. Hope you've got a health club in town so I can work this off tomorrow."

"We don't, but there's a Y in Morgan, the next town over. It's about a twenty-minute drive from here."

Lindy pushed back from the table and stretched her arms over her head. "Sounds good, I'll need something to keep me busy. Matt, I'm beat. Can I have your car keys so I can head back to your place? I'm sure Carrie would be happy to give you a lift home later...or tomorrow morning." A knowing grin curved her lips.

"I'd be happy to give you a ride home," Carrie replied without missing a beat. "If you want to stay for a little while."

Okay, was she saying what he thought she was saying? She met his gaze, but for once, Matt couldn't read her facial expressions. Hell, who was he kidding? Didn't matter why she wanted him to stay, Matt wasn't going anywhere until she kicked his ass out. He pulled his keys from his pocket and tossed them to Lindy. "Think you can find your way back from here?"

"I'll manage." She caught the keys and stood. "Head back to Salvation, make a right, and then another right at the light. Second house on the left."

"Memory like a steel trap," Matt teased. "Make sure the back door's unlocked."

"Will do, big brother. Carrie, thanks for supper and the recipes."

"My pleasure. Good night."

Once Lindy drove off, Carrie got up and retrieved what looked like a small envelope from the top of her microwave and handed it to him. "This is for you."

"A present? But I don't have anything for you."

She gave a teasing eye roll. "Just open it."

Matt arched a brow, peeled the flap open, and shook the envelope over his hand. A key fell out. He looked at her, his heart thumping.

What a huge statement she'd made with just that small gesture. Obviously, this was Carrie's way of letting him know she accepted him as her partner.

"To the coffee shop," she needlessly explained. Matt gave a curt nod, overcome with emotion. He wanted to race around the kitchen table and crush her in his arms, kiss her like she'd never been kissed before…Whoa, buddy, baby steps. He'd started to fear Carrie would never fully trust him—or any man—in this lifetime. If he put the moves on her and she wasn't "there" yet, he'd ruin any chance they had of…of what? Hell, Matt was half in love with her, and for all he knew she thought of him like a big brother.

Then again, a woman didn't put on makeup and wear sexy clothes for her big brother. Hell, if she didn't send out so many mixed signals he'd know which way was up. And all the vibes she sent out were—

"Matt? You all right?"

Carrie gazed at him with a frown of concern. He chuckled, praying like hell she couldn't read minds. Then again, if she could, she'd have slammed the door in his face two seconds after answering it. "Yeah, sorry. Just hoping Lindy made it back to the cottage safe."

"Oh." She sounded disappointed, which confused him even more. "Well, give her a quick call. I need to run upstairs for something anyway."

Carrie raced up the stairs and ran into the bathroom, locking the door behind her. Stupid, stupid, stupid. She shouldn't have presented the key like it was some sort of gift or something. He had as much right to have a key to *Coffee To Chai For* as she did. But the look on his face...almost as if a spider had dropped into his palm, the way he'd gawked at it.

Carrie pushed away from the door and checked herself in the mirror. What he must think, she thought, holding back tears. Normally she didn't bother with makeup, and she rarely wore anything other than the black slacks and the cute T-shirts she sported for work. Tonight she'd taken a chance and prettied herself up. What a joke. Her makeup was so heavy it looked like a child had applied it; her boobs were one good bounce away from freedom, and her tight jeans would leave angry lines that lasted a week.

Okay, so he hadn't flown across the table and kissed her breathless. Certainly not the end of the world. Carrie tore off a piece of toilet paper and dabbed at her eyes. Matt wasn't interested in her that way. She'd read all the signs wrong. And if he were a gentleman, he'd never mention this night again.

After a few deep, calming breaths, she opened the door and headed back downstairs. Matt stood at her kitchen sink gazing out the window. The sun had already started its downward descent, bathing her backyard with its warm, golden glow.

He glanced over his shoulder as she approached, and a welcoming smile transformed his handsome face. Carrie wanted to kiss him something fierce, but she didn't dare. She'd never be able to live down the humiliation if he backed away when she leaned in.

She walked up beside him and looked out into her yard. "So whatcha looking at?"

"You have a hammock."

He said it with such reverence, she was hard-pressed not to laugh. "Yep. My parents started the tradition. This used to be their house. I bought it from them when they moved their practice to Green Bay."

"So you grew up in Redemption then?"

She nodded. "Born and raised. Well, actually, I was born in a hospital in Green Bay, but you know what I mean."

"Can we try it?"

"Huh?"

He chuckled. "The hammock. I've never been on one before. Are they as hard to lie on as they're made out to be?"

He looked so darn hopeful, Carrie wanted to laugh.

"Not once you get the hang of it. Come on." She motioned him to follow her outside and led him toward the two stately oak trees her father estimated were over three hundred years old. The hammock, however, was new. Her father's old Pawley had finally given out after over two decades of service, so Carrie replaced it with a soft as silk, multicolored Mayan without a spreader bar. Heaven.

The sweet scent of petunias filled the air, as did the four o'clocks her mother loved so much, and the night blooming jasmine—Carrie's personal favorite. Her mother had started the night garden when Carrie was still in diapers, and although her time was limited these days, Carrie enjoyed it too much to give it up.

"Smells nice," Matt commented as he fingered one of the many pink, purple, and white blooms that grew up the side of the arched trellis.

"I love it back here. I'll grab a book and lay in the hammock for an hour or so almost every night."

"Sounds like heaven."

Carrie grinned over his choice of words. "That it is. Go ahead, try it."

He looked at her as if she'd just told him to jump into a pit of snakes. "I don't know how."

"Sorry, forgot. It's pretty easy, believe it or not." Carrie positioned herself with her back to the hammock, grabbed it with both hands and sat down, then slowly lay back as she spread the delicate strings out with her hands. "Okay, get in next to me, but not too fast. These types are hard to flip, but you still have to get in it with care. And make sure there's nothing sharp in your back pockets."

"Don't you need to turn? You know, so your head and feet are facing the trees?" He propped his hands on his hips and frowned, eyeing the hammock with hesitancy.

"No, that's why Mayan hammocks are hard to flip."

Matt stared at it for few seconds, shrugged, then turned and slowly lowered himself onto the hammock.

"See? Easy-peasy."

"Are you kidding? You just jinxed me for sure," he said with a laugh.

"Come on, lie back and relax. I'm telling you, once you're sprawled out, you'll never want to get off."

He took a deep breath, as if he were about to dive off a cliff instead of simply lie back on a hammock. "Here goes nothing." He slowly reclined back until he was lying right beside her, shoulder to shoulder, thigh to thigh.

Carrie closed her eyes for a moment as she savored the feel of his warm body pressed against hers. She hadn't been this close to a man in years, close enough to smell his spicy aftershave, feel the hard contours of his muscled arm. God, how she wanted to turn her head and take a whiff of him. She bit back a smile over the absurdity of her thoughts.

"Mind if we get a little more comfy?"

Carrie's pulse picked up speed as Matt carefully maneuvered one arm beneath her and curled her into his side, his hand stroking possessively up and down her side. Her breasts were crushed against his chest, and she wasn't sure, but it felt like one was about to pop out.

"Better?" he asked, his breath warm against her scalp.

A shiver ran through her and her nipples hardened. *Oh, God, oh, God, oh, God.*

"Hey, you all right? I didn't mean to make you uncomfortable. It's just...I've been waiting all week for a chance to get my arms around you."

She tried to lean back and gaze into his eyes, gauge the truth of his words, but it wasn't easy in a hammock. "Really? I kinda thought...but then I wasn't sure..." Great, she sounded like a complete and utter idiot.

He gave a soft chuckle and turned slightly toward her, his lips just inches from her own. The sun had finally disappeared into the western horizon, his handsome face now completely in shadow. "Funny, I've never been more sure of anything." He dropped his voice down to a near whisper. "I'm crazy about you, Carrie. All I can think about right now is kissing you."

"Then why are you still talking?" she whispered back, emboldened by his confession. She tilted her face up, making it clear that she wanted the kiss as much as he did.

Matt didn't waste a second. He captured her mouth with a soft groan, moving gently at first, coaxing a response with his incredibly soft lips. When Carrie parted hers, he deepened the kiss, running his hot tongue along her bottom lip before slipping it past her teeth in search of her own. She met the stroke of his tongue with a sigh of relief. He tasted like pure heaven—chocolate and wine.

Overwhelmed by how right it felt to be in his arms, Carrie slipped one arm up around his neck and opened her mouth a little wider, inviting him to deepen the kiss even more. Matt needed no further persuading. He wrapped his other arm around her and crushed her against his chest, his hands kneading her back, her waist, and finally wandering down to cup her backside, pressing her into his hardness.

A familiar ache flared to life just below her bellybutton. It'd been so long since she'd felt sexual attraction, she'd started to wonder if her sex drive had died along with her marriage. But oh no, her body was practically singing for Matt's touch. She draped one leg over his hip, and the hammock flipped over.

Chapter Six

———⚬———

They landed on the soft grass in a tangle of limbs, their feet twisted in the fine, hand-woven netting. The initial shock wore off after a couple of heartbeats and then they both burst out laughing.

Matt managed to disentangle her feet first, then his own. Once they were both standing, he took her back into his arms. "Hard to flip, huh?"

Carrie laughed softly, her eyes closed as she inhaled his wonderful scent. "I said hard, not impossible. Be thankful I use fertilizer; the grass is as soft as a pillow-top mattress.

"And do you own a pillow-top mattress?" His breath whispered across her ear, turning her knees to Jell-O.

Carrie's heart was so full she thought she might float away like a helium balloon. For the first time in so long she couldn't remember, her guard was down and her mind open. She'd lumped most men into the same despicable category for years, but thanks to Matt she'd finally started to believe in the opposite sex again. That maybe, just maybe, she wouldn't wind up as some bitter old cat lady. "You may very well find out, but it won't be tonight. I'm not that easy."

He pulled back and cupped her cheeks, his thumbs stroking gently under her chin, his gorgeous face illuminated by the moonlight. "I'd have been disappointed had you invited me in to find out."

Liar. She grinned. "Yeah, right. You're just saying what you think I want to hear."

He reached up and caressed her face, traced his thumb across her bottom lip. "I'm a hundred percent serious. As much as I want you—and Carrie, I've never wanted a woman more—the first time we make love is going to be perfect. And, no, I'm not just saying what I think you want to hear."

Carrie could hear the humor in his voice, but also the sincerity. Somehow, she knew he meant every word, and the thought excited her like nothing else. She slid her arms up around his neck and pulled him down for a second kiss. Matt slanted his mouth across hers and crushed her to him. As their lips and tongues meshed with hungry need, Carrie couldn't stop thinking about her comfy pillow-top mattress.

By the time Matt tore his lips from hers, she could barely think straight. He gave her one last kiss on the forehead. "This night has been incredible. I haven't been so happy in...I don't know how long. But if I don't leave now, I can't promise my good intentions will hold out."

"And I can't promise I wouldn't change my mind about being easy," she admitted, only half joking, as she grasped his hand and led him back into the house. They rode to Matt's house in comfortable silence. Carrie had plenty on her mind to keep her thoughts occupied, and she supposed Matt did as well. She decided to walk him to his back door, which got a chuckle out of him.

"I can honestly say this is a first; a woman walking me to the door."

She backed him up against the vinyl siding, then smoothed her hands up his chest and around his neck. "You know, I've never really been the jealous type, but I'm very glad to be your first."

Matt slid his hands into her back pockets and pulled her flush against him. Carrie gasped as the proof of his desire burned against her belly. "I'm going to be your first for a lot of things, Carrie. Most importantly, I'm going to be the first man to not let you down. You can trust me, sweetheart. I swear it."

Carrie's heart did a funny little flip. More than anything she wanted to believe him. Believe in him. But she had to be realistic. They'd barely known each other, really known each other, a week. "I get that you mean what you say, but—"

Matt stopped her words with a searing kiss. When he lifted his head, he said, "No buts. Have a little faith, Carrie. Believe in us."

All she had the strength to do was nod, floored by his choice of words. More than anything she wanted to trust him. And darn it, that's exactly what she planned to do. She'd suffered enough at her ex-husband's hands; no way would she let him rob her of a possible future with a wonderful, honest man like Matt Jacobs.

"I do," she said, and meant it. "I trust you." She wrapped her arms around his waist and leaned against his chest. The beat of his heart was comforting, reassuring. "So, should I plan to see you bright and early tomorrow, or do you plan to sleep in?" she teased.

"Actually, I have to drive Lindy into Green Bay tomorrow. She wants to hit the YMCA for an hour or so, then have lunch in town. And to finish the day off, she'll probably drag me to the nearest mall."

Carrie mumbled an "Oh, okay," against his chest, but truthfully, her throat was thick with disappointment. She'd imagined they'd spend the morning working side by side, and since Matt didn't work weekends at the library, she figured he'd probably stay and close the shop with her for the first time. Maybe discuss the new menu they had in the works.

Then she'd invite him back to her place, cook him supper again...something healthier this time. Wait, what the heck was she doing? She may not follow some strict diet, but she ate plenty of fresh fruits and vegetables, drank tons of water, took vitamins religiously. Probably why she was always so frustrated by those extra fifteen pounds she couldn't seem to shed no matter what she tried. Okay, true, she'd never been much for working out. Maybe it was time she started jogging or something.

Yeah, right, she thought with a mental snort. There wasn't a bra made that could hold her boobs down so she could run comfortably.

Matt kissed her on the top of the head and unhooked her arms from around his neck. "I'd better get inside while I still can. It's hard to think straight when you're this close."

"I know the feeling."

He grinned. "Any chance we can get together Sunday?"

"I'd like that. Supper again, my place? You bring the movie?"

"Deal."

"I feel like I've died and gone to heaven," Matt declared, as he forked up a huge bit of lasagna. "You're a fantastic cook."

Carrie tipped her wineglass at him. "And you can lie with a straight face. Good to know." She gave him a cheeky grin. "Seriously, thanks. I've learned a lot living next to Lauren. She can make something like Coq au Vin one night, and tater tot casserole the next. So I have quite a mix of recipes saved up."

Matt gazed across the table, unable to take his eyes off of her. Corny as it sounded, she became more and more beautiful to him every day. She'd sleeked her gorgeous, shiny, long hair back in a ponytail, emerald teardrop earrings hung from her ears, and a matching necklace nestled in her cleavage. She wore a powder blue baby-doll T-shirt tonight, the light shade really making the deeper blue of her eyes stand out. "I like tater tot casserole," he said, having no clue what it was. Somehow he knew he'd like it.

"I'll keep that in mind."

They ate in silence for awhile. Matt couldn't remember the last time he'd wolfed down so much food. Since they planned to veg out in front of the TV, he really wasn't concerned with physical activity for the next few hours. Heck, maybe she'd offer to rub his belly. The thought brought a smile to his face.

"What's so funny?"

He almost laughed out loud. "Nothing. Just thinking about Lindy."

Carrie popped the last of her breadstick into her mouth and washed it down with a mouthful of wine.

"That's right, I forgot to ask. How was your trip into Green Bay? Did Lindy enjoy herself?" She refilled her glass and gazed at him with those mesmerizing blue eyes.

Matt watched her, wanting nothing more than to leap across the table and kiss her soundly. He managed to control himself, but it was a near thing. "She did. Thought the city was magnificent. Wanted to cruise around the older sections of town and check out the homes. Practically bounced in her seat when we discovered a beautiful old church on the east side of town. She even took pictures of it…which was a little out of character, but fun to watch." He took a quick sip of his wine. "Let's see…Oh, we rode past Lambeau Field, even though Lindy can't stand football. Just seemed sacrilegious not to."

"It really is," Carrie confirmed in all seriousness. Then she grinned and took another sip of her wine. "Bounced in her seat? I don't know. Somehow I can't picture that."

"Nonetheless, it's true. Can't remember the last time I saw her so excited."

She giggled. "'Nonetheless'. Who even uses that word?"

"I just did. And it's a perfectly good word, smartass." God, how she enchanted him. He needed to keep his thoughts PG, or things could get incredibly uncomfortable on the sofa.

She shot him a saucy look before getting up to clear the table. Matt jumped to his feet to help. By the time he escorted her into the living room, she could barely keep her hands to herself. She tried to pull him down on the sofa with her, but Matt needed to pop the movie into the DVD player—thankfully, because he also needed to cool the hell down or he'd never make it through the movie.

But he did need her to sleep soundly tonight. If she woke up too early in the morning, it would ruin the surprise he had planned.

"I could use a refill before I start the movie. You?"

She tipped her glass back and drained it. "Yep. Just bring the bottle. You know, believe it or not, I haven't had anything to drink in almost two years."

"Oh, I believe it," he teased, wondering why she felt the need for such fortification tonight. He retrieved the bottle, grabbed the remote off the coffee table, and plopped down next to her on the sofa. Carrie leaned into him and snuggled against his side.

Matt was a happy camper, no doubt about it. He hit play. "Hope you like what I picked out."

"I'm sure I will. I love movies." She craned her neck to peer up at him. "Unless it's a Kung Fu movie. Hate those."

Matt chuckled. He could stare into those big blue eyes all night long. "No Kung Fu. It's a comedy. And I'm glad you like movies, I'm a bit of a buff myself." She smiled and snuggled into his lap. Matt prayed for strength as he took the wineglass from her hands and set it on the table. "So, how was your day yesterday? Did the Whitman order finally arrive?"

She let out a delicate yawn, nodding as she did. Surprising since it was barely six thirty in the evening. And if she passed out now, she'd never sleep late in the morning.

He tried to get her to sit up a little. "Come on, sweetheart, you don't plan to fall asleep on me, do you? The movie's about to start."

"No, sorry, I'm good. I stayed up late reading last night. It's been awhile since I read a book so good I couldn't put it down."

"You know, for all the reading you do, I think I've seen you in the library once."

A sheepish grin pursed her lips. "I buy a new book every week at the grocery store. A habit I picked up from my mother."

"I can think of a lot worse habits."

The previews finally ended, and Carrie let out an adorable squeal when she realized what movie he'd rented. "I love Night at the Museum." She sat up a little straighter, wrapping both her arms around one of his. "Ben Stiller's a riot."

Matt gave her a peck on the forehead. "Glad you like it. It's not exactly a new release, but I was hoping you hadn't seen it yet."

"I've watched it with Lauren and the kids several times. "She looked up at him and said in a deep voice, "Hey, Dum-Dum, you got gum-gum?"

Matt burst out laughing and Carrie did, too. Her face grew pink, and he wasn't sure if it was embarrassment, the wine, or both.

Although he cursed the circumstances that had brought him to Redemption, in an odd way he almost wished it'd happened years ago so he could've met Carrie sooner. Maybe they'd be married by now, have a couple of kids.

Whoa…holy shit. Married with kids? Matt took a healthy gulp of his wine.

"Carrie?"

"Hmm?"

"Tell me about your ex-husband."

Chapter Seven

Slowly, she sat up and stared at him. "Buzz kill. I don't wanna talk about him. Ever." Matt reached out and traced his finger down her cheek, but she pulled back and scooched into the corner. "Carrie, we have to talk about him. I mean, look how just the mention of him sets you off."

She stared at the TV, stubbornly silent. Just when he'd decided to drop the subject, she said, "Not much to tell, really. We met in high school, he was a bad boy, I fell hard and fast. Before I knew it, we were married and miserable. He, uh, wasn't a very nice guy."

Matt stilled, afraid of the answer to his next question. "Did he hurt you?"

She gave a bitter laugh. "You could say that."

He gently coaxed her back into his arms. She resisted for all of two seconds. "You can tell me, Carrie. You can trust me, I swear."

She gazed up at him, and her face fell; tears filled her eyes. She angrily swiped them away. "I'm sorry, I don't mean to be a baby. I just try not to think about that time in my life. It's over and done with. He moved down to Madison, opened his own coffee shop. I'll never have to look at his face again, and that's good enough for me."

"Sweetheart, what did the bastard do to you?"

"What didn't he do? He was evil. Well, supposedly he had a chemical imbalance, which his mother decided to share with me after I'd married the nut. They moved to town when we were in tenth grade. Charlie and Drew were in a couple of classes with him, and I was friends with Drew's girlfriend, so we all hung out together.

"I know this is going to seem hard to believe, but he never laid a hand on me until after we were married. And once he started...well, it just got worse and worse."

Matt had to take deep breaths to keep his anger in check. He massaged her neck with gentle pressure.

She snatched her wineglass off the coffee table for a couple of quick sips. "I've never told anyone the whole story before."

"You don't have to...I had no right—"

"No, I want to." She set her glass down and leaned back. "It's just...hard. And embarrassing. He started hitting me about a month into the marriage. For stupid stuff like forgetting to buy bread when I was at the store, or not washing his favorite jeans."

"Didn't anyone realize something was wrong? Your brothers? Charlie and Drew?"

She gave her head a vehement shake. "I was careful, acted blissfully happy whenever anyone was around. Charlie suspected, but I swore everything was fine. I managed to keep it a secret for over four years."

"Jesus." He crushed her to him, stunned to learn she'd endured four years of abuse— physical and emotional—before anyone figured it out.

"Sometimes it seems like yesterday," she admitted against his cheek. "And I'm not proud of some of the thoughts I had back then." She pulled back and faced him, the desolation in her eyes breaking his heart. "The last time Rob hit me, Charlie showed up. Rob had me by the hair and was slamming my head against the fridge when the back door burst open. Charlie beat the hell out of him, and then got me out of there. Rob decided to press charges and used some...pictures he'd taken of me to force my hand."

Matt was afraid he knew exactly what kind of pictures the pig had held over her head. "You don't have to tell me."

Tears welled in her eyes again and she looked away. "We were newlyweds, it was our friggin' honeymoon. Yes, I let him take some nude pictures of me. I trusted him, he was my husband. It's not like—"

"Carrie, you don't have to justify yourself to me. I'm not judging you. I've even developed a little respect for Charlie."

"He saved me from major head trauma—maybe saved my life—and for that, I'll always be grateful. And he knew I didn't want anyone to know about the abuse, especially my family. They'd always hated Rob. My parents are the ones who bought me *Coffee To Chai For*. They drew up papers, ironclad papers that stated if Rob and I ever divorced, he wouldn't have any claim to it, which pissed him off big time." She took a deep, fortifying breath before continuing.

"So he threatened to not only put Charlie in jail, but to make those pictures public—in town, on the Internet—if I didn't give him half the worth of *Coffee To Chai For* in cash. That's why I can barely pay my bills. I have a mortgage over my head on top of my house payment and the costs of running a business. And I would've rather died than let anyone find out about those pictures. Especially my mom and dad. They warned me back in high school that Rob was no good, but of course, I didn't listen."

"You wouldn't be the first teenager to disregard your parents' warnings."

"I know." She let out a deep sigh. "But if I only had, you know?"

She grew quiet and curled up in his lap again. He had a feeling the confession had taken as much out of her physically as it had emotionally. Matt stroked her back as they watched the movie. When she didn't laugh over the 'Dum-Dum' line, he wondered if she'd fallen asleep.

When the credits started rolling, she surprised him by sitting up and twining her arms around his neck. Her gaze hovered on his mouth. "Kiss me, Matt. Please. I need you."

Christ, not nearly as much as he needed her. Matt brushed a lock of hair from her eyes and gently cupped the side of her face. Raw emotion tightened his chest as he brought his mouth down on hers. He kissed her reverently, careful not to take more than she was willing to give. This amazing woman had been through so much, had endured such horrific abuse at the hand of her ex that Matt was somewhat fearful of making her feel rushed or uncomfortable. But when she slung one leg over his lap and plastered herself against him, he was lost.

He slid his tongue past her lips, swallowing her soft sigh as he kissed the beautiful woman in his arms with everything he had. He stroked and caressed her with great care, wanting her to know how extraordinary she was, how much he desired her. He traced the line of her jaw, the column of her throat, following his hand with his lips.

Carrie arched her neck, allowing him better access as she did a little exploring of her own, running her hands over his shoulders, kneading softly before moving down his arms, driving him crazy with just those soft caresses. She slipped her hands beneath his shirt and pressed her palms against his chest. After a quick nip of his earlobe, she whispered, "Matt, I want you. So much."

He dropped his head back against the sofa and regarded her with thoughtful concern. Hard and aching, Matt wanted nothing more than to strip her naked and make love to her until neither of them could move. But he feared her sudden need for him had more to do with his forcing her to talk about her ex than being ready to take things to the next level.

"Sweetheart, I want you, too. More than I can put into words. But—"

She leaned in a kissed him silent. When she pulled back, she shook her head and whispered, "No 'but'. I want you, and if the iron rod wedged between us is any indication, you want me, too. Don't deny it."

Christ, she was going to be the death of him. "I'm not denying anything. It's just...Look, I made you talk about things that brought up painful memories. Made you feel vulnerable and needy."

She arched a brow. "Needy?"

Shit. "I didn't mean it like that. I just meant....Ah, hell, I'm afraid to say anything else or I might cram my other foot in my mouth."

Carrie gave him a playful tap on the nose. "Good call. Just keep your sexy mouth shut until I say otherwise, and we'll get along fine."

"Do I have to worry about you pulling out whips and chains?" he teased.

She laughed, the sound beautiful music to his ears. "I may be adventurous, but I like to stay on this side of kinky, if that's all right with you."

He winked. "You're in charge here, Carrie. I'm merely your willing slave, eager to serve you in any way you wish."

"I love a man who knows his place," she purred before leaning in to nip at his bottom lip. And damn if his heart didn't start thumping with anticipation.

She pressed her lips to his again, this time opening up to him as she tugged his shirt free and started working it up his chest. She broke the kiss only long enough to pull his shirt over his head, their mouths meshing hungrily again as she tossed it on the floor. Matt plumbed her hot mouth, every inch of him hard with need. She tasted of wine, and Matt savored the heady flavor as she kissed him with more passion than any woman ever had.

Desperate to feel her soft flesh, Matt slipped his hands beneath her shirt, her hot skin nearly scorching his palms. He cupped her breasts over her bra, and she arched into him with a sexy little gasp. He massaged the large globes, teasing her nipples through the lacey material, reveling in how perfect she was for him; how she epitomized every fantasy he'd ever had of the perfect woman. Carrie Lowell couldn't be more ideal for him if she'd been custom made.

She caught her bottom lip between her teeth as she reached back to unclasp her bra. Matt wasted no time in slipping beneath it to palm the soft, supple flesh in his greedy palms. She peeled her own shirt off and tossed it aside, then her bra, as Matt paid loving homage to the most beautiful pair he'd ever seen. She braced her hands on the sofa behind him, her head falling back as Matt tongued first one pebbled peak; circling, flicking, lapping, sucking, before paying equal loving attention to her other breast. The thought of bringing her to orgasm with his mouth tightened his groin and nearly sent him over the edge. He wanted to pleasure her thoroughly, worship her, make damn sure she didn't doubt his devotion for even a second.

Putting his own needs on the backburner, Matt stood and switched their positions, settling Carrie on the sofa while he kneeled before her. With her cheeks flushed, her lips plump from his kisses, and those bountiful breasts with their pretty pink tips wet from his mouth, Carrie had never looked more desirable to him. He made quick work of stripping off the rest of her clothes, and within seconds she lay naked and open before him.

"You're incredible," he whispered. "So damn beautiful."

Before she had a chance to respond, Matt gripped her by the hips and pulled her to the edge of the cushion. Not sure what to expect, if she would be open to what he so badly wanted to do to her, or uncomfortable, he wasn't surprised when she attempted to rise and switch places with him.

"I want to be on top," she whispered, clutching the waistband of his jeans and popping the button free.

Matt's pulse faltered as he grasped her hands and kissed them. The thought of her riding him, those magnificent breasts bouncing, her head thrown back, was just about more than he could take. Steeling his resolve, he coaxed her back into the position he wanted.

"And I want that, too, sweetheart. There are so many things I want to do with you. Do to you." He splayed his hands on the tender skin of her thighs and smiled at her slight quiver.

"But I'm supposed to be in charge," she pouted in a throaty purr.

"Then tell me what you want me to do." He punctuated his words with a gentle squeeze.

"Tell me how to please you. Because Carrie, all I can think about right now is tasting you."

Another shiver told him exactly how his words had affected her. Carrie was a deeply sensual woman who'd been hiding behind fear and bitterness for far too long. As if reading his mind, she smiled her consent and grasped his hands. Matt held her heavy-lidded gaze as she guided him to her core.

And Matt didn't waste a second. He brushed his fingers through her tights curls, watching as she tugged that luscious bottom lip between her teeth—a gesture he found incredibly sexy. She clutched the sofa cushion with both hands and trembled as he slid one finger between her wet folds.

Her head fell back again as he opened her, and a small cry escaped her when he circled her swollen bead. Her arousal was a beautiful thing to watch, her scent so seductive. Matt clenched his teeth, afraid he'd embarrass himself before he'd even had her on his tongue. He slid his other hand beneath her butt and squeezed, drawing another moan from her. She released the cushion and cupped her breasts, kneading them as she continued to hold his gaze.

Damn, she was magnificent. He slid one finger into her tight channel and leaned in to lap at her tight bud. She arched into him with another soft purr. Sliding his other hand beneath her bottom, he lifted her off the sofa, powerless to hold back, pleasuring her with his tongue before covering her with his mouth and sucking hard.

She cried out, her hips arching as she came, her fingers tunneling through his hair and gripping so hard it'd be a miracle if she didn't yank a clump out. Matt didn't care or ease up, his lips and tongue working to wring every last groan from her until she went limp with a lusty sigh of contentment. Matt smiled with satisfaction as he rose up to face her.

"Pretty damn pleased with yourself, aren't you?" she said, her contented smile in direct contrast with her teasing demand.

"Yep."

She giggled as he stood up and unbuttoned his jeans, making quick work of stripping them off, along with his boxer briefs and socks. Carrie surprised him by grabbing his hand and pulling him down beside her on the sofa. She straddled his lap and pinned his shoulders to the sofa, making it quite clear she was taking over. Matt smiled with anticipation.

Carrie held his gaze with more confidence than she felt. Though she'd never been shy, she was certainly no sex kitten either. But she wanted this man more than she wanted air; just the *thought* of him buried deep inside her was more stimulating than anything she'd ever experienced.

She leaned in and kissed him on the mouth, teasing him with the tip of her tongue as she wrapped her fingers around his hard length. She gave a gentle squeeze, amazed by the contrast of silky smooth over solid steel. He groaned, a drawn out, sexy male rumbling that heightened her excitement. She moved up and down his erection with sure strokes, eager to please him, eager to make him come apart as thoroughly as he had her.

"Do you have protection?" she asked. "I do, but it's upstairs."

He stopped her hand with a pained chuckle. "Another few seconds of that and we won't even need any." He leaned over and rustled around in his jeans pocket before pulling out his wallet. Extracting two condoms he admitted, "I picked these up in Green Bay."

"Feeling confident, were you?"

"Hopeful," he corrected, handing her the condoms. "With a little wishful thinking thrown in."

With a coquettish smile, Carrie accepted the condoms and set one on the end table. She slid off the sofa and crouched before him. He spread his thighs a bit as if in anticipation. Carrie grasped his stiff sex and leaned in to tease the head with the tip of her tongue. Matt watched her through half-mast eyes, a slow smile curving his lips, as she tasted him, running her tongue from tip to base, licking every inch of his impressive length before taking him into her mouth. She loved the taste of him, the sexy, musky scent that was purely Matt.

He arched into her with a low groan, his voice thick as he whispered, "God, yes."

Feeling empowered, Carrie sat up and tore the condom wrapper open, then slowly, lovingly, sheathed him. Matt gripped her hip with one hand and held his thick sex with the other as she slowly sank down his hard length. Carrie could barely hold his gaze as they came together for the first time with a mutual groan of satisfaction. Nothing had ever felt so right to her, so perfect as he stretched her to the limit.

Once she became more comfortable, Carrie moved with confidence, riding him with slow sure strokes, her hands braced on the back of the sofa. Matt caressed her breasts, her ribcage, her lower back. Their breathing grew labored as their pace quickened. Suddenly, he broke the kiss and clasped her bottom with both hands, thrusting inside her as their need grew to a fevered pitch.

Carrie cried out, her release quick and earth-shattering. She continued to ride him until a hoarse shout tore from his own throat. Their bodies strained together as they crested each and every sweet wave. Carrie collapsed on top of him, the smile stretching her cheeks so huge she could hardly contain it. Had she ever been this happy, felt this comfortable with another living soul?

Still inside her, Matt stood up and headed for the stairs. Laughing, Carrie grabbed the bottle of wine off the table and held on for dear life.

They talked, kissed, and caressed each other as they finished the bottle of wine, making love twice more before falling asleep wrapped in each other's arms. Carrie's last thought before dozing off was that she'd finally found a man worthy of trust.

Sunlight streamed through the vertical blinds, washing Carrie's face with warmth. Yawning, she stretched lazily before flipping onto her stomach. Memories of the night before flooded her mind, and her eyes popped open. She turned, expecting to find Matt slumbering beside her. Only the space next to her was empty. She lifted her head to glance around the room. Where the hell was he?

A wave of nausea rolled through her as she sat up, and a slight pounding started in the back of her skull. Crap…they'd sucked down a whole bottle of wine, plus she'd polished off the last bottle while cooking supper. Carrie plopped back down on the pillow and gingerly massaged her temples. She couldn't remember the last time she'd been hungover, and as needles of agony stabbed her brain, she swore off booze for good.

When the intense brightness of the sun finally registered on her foggy consciousness, she sat up again with a start. Holy shit, she'd overslept!

She tossed back the covers and raced into the bathroom. After a quick shower, she called the shop, praying Matt was there and that everything was all right. Not once since the day she'd opened *Coffee To Chai For* had she overslept, and she silently cursed herself as she waited for him to pick up. When he didn't answer by the eighth ring, she tried his cell phone. No answer on his cell either.

Starting to panic, she grabbed her purse and keys and ran out the door, casting a quick glance at a small beige car she'd never seen before parked across the street, its occupants openly staring at her. Huh. She resisted the urge to flip them off, jumped in her car, and drove away.

A quick glance in her rearview mirror told her they were following right behind. Her anger dissipated somewhat as uneasiness took its place. Who the hell were they and what did they want with her? Doing her best to ignore them, she turned onto Salvation Avenue...and got the shock of her life. Her parking lot was filled with a construction team!

No. Matt wouldn't have made such a monumental decision without consulting her, and she'd already made it clear she needed to think on it. But as she approached her shop there was no denying what her lying eyes were seeing. The west friggin' wall was missing!

Carrie squealed to a stop in front of the shop, bound from her car, and stormed to the front door. She nearly had a coronary when she read the sign taped to the glass: Closed One Week For Remodeling. Her blood pressure spiked. That sneaky rat bastard, she was going to kill him! Did he honestly think he could make such a huge decision without her? Well, of course he did—he had.

But wait, she'd only given him the key Friday night. How could he have had a crew here that fast? Could he have met with them on Saturday when he was in Green Bay with his sister? Or maybe they hadn't gone to Green Bay at all. Cursing, she yanked open the door and stormed inside. Matt stood talking to one of the workers, and Lindy sat on the counter sipping from a *Coffee To Chai For* cup. Carrie stalked toward Matt, yanking Lindy off the counter as she passed.

"Hey, what the hell! You made me spill my cappuccino!"

Carrie didn't so much as spare her a glance. When she reached Matt's side—who still hadn't noticed her thanks to the noisy machinery—she grabbed his arm. "I need to speak with you. Now."

Matt spoke a few words to the guy, thumped him on the back, and then turned to face her. He frowned, as if he had no clue what her problem was. "You don't look as well-rested as I'd imagined. Which isn't helping my ego right now." He winked, then glanced around them. "I guess it's a little late to yell 'surprise.'"

And then he grinned. The jackass actually grinned.

"What the hell is going on here? How dare you make such an enormous decision without my okay!"

"Just calm down and let me explain," he said, trying to take her in his arms.

Carrie stiff-armed him and took a step back. "Don't you dare touch me. You knew I wasn't ready for this, so you waited until I was weak and vulnerable—you slept with me—and then did whatever the hell you wanted. And I played right into your hands when I gave you that key!"

He propped his hands on his hips and frowned. "Don't you think you're overreacting just a little? I mean, yeah, maybe I should've gotten your okay before having them start the job, but sweetheart, I'm doing this for you. I want this place to become the hottest lunch spot in Redemption so you never have to worry about money again."

Carrie gazed up at him, her anger slowly dissipating even though she tried to hang onto it for dear life. Without it, she was putty in his hands, and she swore a long time ago she'd never give another man that kind of power over her.

Matt reached out again, and this time she let him take her in his arms. "Look, I know I deserve your anger, but I swear, by the time this place is done, you're going to love it. The drive-thru alone is going to double your business, and with a larger dining room you'll be able to accommodate a pretty decent lunch and early supper crowd."

He was right and she knew it. Change was always scary, but since the change was already in motion, somehow it seemed a little less daunting. "I don't want Lindy's ass on my counter," she mumbled against his chest.

Matt laughed. "Sweetheart, there's not another woman in the world like you."

Carrie headed behind the counter and made herself a cappuccino with a double shot of espresso. Lindy had parked herself back on the counter, and as Carrie and Matt strode past, Matt picked his sister up and settled her on a chair. Carrie laughed as they walked outside into the morning sunshine, Lindy on their heels.

"What's your problem, both of you? I was simply minding my own business, watching the guys work. Not much else to do here in Mayberry."

Before Matt or Carrie could respond, a couple of car doors slammed, and she looked up to see those same two men rushing toward them brandishing cameras. Carrie blinked in surprise. Reporters coming to do a piece about the coffee shop? Already? But why had they been parked in front of her house?

Lindy grasped Carrie's arm and tried to pull her back into the shop while Matt hurried forward and met the reporters in the street.

"Let go," Carrie snapped, yanking free of Lindy's hold. "What the hell are you doing? Do you know those guys?"

"I know their type," Lindy muttered. "Believe me, for your own sake, get inside your shop and lock the door."

A bad feeling mushroomed in Carrie's gut. She stood and watched as the reporters skirted past Matt and beelined straight for her. Matt grabbed one of them by the arm and yanked him around. "I'm warning you, get back in your car and get the hell outta here!"

"Matt? What in the world—"

"Ms. Lowell," the second reporter shouted as a flashbulb popped in her face. "How does it feel to be dating an accused murderer?"

"An accused murderer? Are you high? Get that thing out of my face."

Matt shoved the other reporter to the ground and his camera crashed beneath him.

"You're gonna pay for that, Spalding! I'm just doing my job—"

Spalding?

"You're a leech who makes his living off other people's misery." Matt pulled some cash from his pocket and threw it on the ground. "Now get the hell out of my sight."

The second reporter continued to snap pictures. Matt started toward him, but he dashed around, keeping out of Matt's reach. "Ms. Lowell, are you aware that you're dating one of the richest men in the country?"

Chapter Eight

𝒞arrie's gaze went from the reporter, to Matt and Lindy—who both sported a deer-in-the-headlights looks—then back to the reporter. "Someone want to tell me what's going on?"

Matt took a step toward her, his expression grave, scaring the hell out of her. "Carrie, can we just head to your place and talk? I think—"

The reporter snapped some more pictures. "This is Jacob Spalding Jr., heir to Spalding Industries, the largest family-owned company in the U.S. He was also the main suspect in the Amanda Ames murder case."

Carrie's heart hammered in her chest. Matt was the guy who'd been wrongly accused of killing Amanda Ames? Carrie remembered hearing on the news how Amanda's supposed lover had been the main suspect, but she couldn't have picked Jacob Spalding out of a lineup if her life depended on it.

"And I was proven innocent. Now grab your friend and get your sorry asses out of my sight before you both need to be hauled away in an ambulance."

The reporter with the smashed camera climbed to his feet and raced back to the car, the second reporter hot on his heels. Once they were safely inside, Smashed Camera guy shouted, "Your days of hiding are over, Spalding. By tonight, everyone will know you've moved on to small-town women. Ms. Lowell, I'd sleep with the light on if I were you."

Matt cursed and gave chase, but the car sped off down the road. He kicked angrily at a rock, cursed again, then turned to face her.

Carrie's heart sunk to the bottom of her stomach. Matt was actually some rich guy named Jacob Spalding...and had been suspected of murder? She stared at him, silently begging him to assure her none of it was true. This was Matt, her Matt, not some rich business type who...who could pay a construction company enough money to start work on a job in two days' time. Who could afford to buy into a business on a librarian's salary, with no home to put up as collateral when he'd been in town less than a year.

"Carrie, listen to me," he said, beseeching her with his eyes. "I would've told you everything, I planned to soon, but then Lindy showed up and I...I panicked."

"Hey," Lindy complained, "don't you dare blame this on me."

"Go away, Lindy."

Brother and sister glared at each other for a moment before Lindy took off in a huff.

"Matt...or should I call you Jacob?" Carrie could hear the bitterness in her own voice. He'd been lying since the moment he'd arrived in town. He'd changed his name, probably changed his appearance, all so he could...what? He could dupe her into bed? It seemed farfetched even to her, but what else could someone that rich and famous want with a "Mayberry" local like her?

"My name is Jacob Matthew Spalding, and I've been called Matt since the day I was born."

"Is that your real hair color? Your real eye color? I mean, how could you have lived in this town all these months without someone recognizing you?"

"Please don't build this up into something bigger than it is. Yes, I lied about my name, but I had good reason. I'd been accused of the most heinous crime imaginable, my family had been under the public's scrutiny for months thanks to me, stocks had gone down, the paparazzi hounded me nonstop. I mean, it was bad enough having them follow me around to clubs and such, but they were suddenly everywhere, and I couldn't take it anymore. I needed to get out of L.A. before I lost my damn mind. Hell, I'd submitted to DNA testing, I was cleared of all charges, and the bloodhounds *still* wouldn't leave me alone."

"How can I believe anything you say? I have no idea who you even are."

"I'm the same man you've known all this time. The same man who's crazy about you, who would do anything for you. Carrie, the last couple weeks, getting to know you—last night—has been the happiest time of my life."

Gazing into those amazing brown eyes, Carrie could easily believe anything he said. Matt was as charming a man as she'd ever known…yet lies fell from his mouth with an ease that startled her. And she'd sold half of her precious business to him. My God, what had she done? She was a complete and utter idiot.

"I should've known," she said, more to herself than him. "You'd think I'd have radar after what I went through with Rob. Jesus, you must've had yourself a big ol' laugh when you left my bed last night. You duped the poor little 'Mayberry' girl"— she made air quotes—"out of half her business. Pretty soon you would have figured out a way to get me to sign over my half. Heck, you probably own half the town by now, don't you?"

He took a step forward. "That's ridiculous and you know it. Now that you know who I am and my family's resources, you must realize your little coffee shop is—"

"Is what? Not worth your time? Good, then sign it back to me and get the hell out of my life. In fact, get the hell out of Redemption."

He crossed his arms over his chest. His eyes grew dark, angry. "I'm not going anywhere, and whether you like it or not, *Coffee To Chai For* is half mine."

Bastard. "There you go, showing your real colors. But you forget, my sister and both my parents are lawyers. I'm sure together they can find a loophole to get me out of our contract."

He closed the distance between them until they were practically nose to nose. She wanted him to kiss her so bad she feared her knees might give out, and she hated herself for the weakness. "And you forget I have the means to keep this in court for a very long time."

Tears burned her eyes. How could she have ever thought this man was decent and kind? "I hate you. You're a despicable excuse for a human being." She gave his chest a jabbing shove, but all the big bully did was grab her by the shoulders.

"You don't mean that. You're just angry—"

"Oh, yes, I do mean it. I'm through. We're through. If my family can't get me out of our contract, you can buy me out. Either way, I never want to see you again. Now let go of me unless you want to add batterer to your list as well."

That seemed to have the desired effect. He released her and stepped back, looking around uncomfortably as if he didn't quite know what to do. Obviously, Mr. Jacob Spalding wasn't used to being put in his place. She gave him one last scathing look, then turned and walked away.

"I'm in love with you, Carrie."

She stopped dead in her tracks and whirled around. Her chest ached as if it would explode. "So, when threats and intimidation don't work, you try the love card? What did you think I'd do, burst into tears and run into your open arms? Not in this lifetime. And just so you know, for the next sucker who falls for your nerdy librarian act, it would've worked better the other way around. Love before threats and intimidation." Carrie turned and strode away, and this time he let her.

"She'll come around," Lindy promised as she poured Matt a glass of wine. "It's a lot for a small-town girl to take in, that the guy she's been dating is rich and powerful."

Matt swirled the burgundy liquid in the glass before taking a cautious sip. He loved his sister dearly, but some days he found it hard to believe they were blood related. "Carrie doesn't give a damn about my money. Besides, her parents are prominent attorneys, Carrie's never wanted for anything."

Lindy sat down across from him and took a sip of the wine she'd picked up at the Piggly Wiggly. Her eyes scrunched and her lips puckered. "Blech. Are you kidding me? How do you drink this crud?"

"I don't, I drink beer. With a bottle of Michelob, I always know what to expect."

He got up and carried his wineglass over to gaze out the kitchen window. His own backyard was barren, without a single flower or shrub to break the monotony.

Yesterday he'd had such big plans in store— a pair of apple trees, a flower garden that would knock Carrie's socks off, a hammock, just like hers. Today he'd decided to put the house on the market. The two-bedroom cottage style home had cost him a song less than a year ago, and he knew he could easily sell it for the same. He didn't care about making a profit. All that mattered was getting the hell out of Redemption.

"Cheer up, big brother. If she doesn't come to her senses, it's her loss. I mean, I'm sorry, but she'd be crazy to let you go. And I'm not just saying that because I'm the best sister in the world."

She flashed him a grin, the same grin that had managed to coax him out of many a bad mood. Unfortunately, the grin didn't do much good against a broken heart.

He heard a car pull into his driveway and spun around. Hope filled his chest, and he stepped over to the side window to glance outside. His heart dropped when he saw a black stretch limo parked behind his Jeep. He set his wineglass on the counter and met Lindy's questioning look. "Mom and Dad are here."

"No way." Lindy rushed to his side and looked for herself. "I can't believe it. After all these months, they finally decide to find you?"

Matt picked up his wineglass and drained it. "My guess would be they're here for you. Probably afraid I'll brainwash you into staying."

She let out a delicate snort. "As if."

Matt took a deep breath and swiped his fingers through his hair before following Lindy outside to greet their parents. The driver got out and opened the door. First his mother stepped out of the vehicle, looking as lovely as ever—a slightly older version of Lindy. She glanced at the house, an oddly wistful note in her eyes, before settling her gaze on Matt. He hadn't seen his mother's beautiful face, hadn't heard her voice in months, and all he wanted to do was throw himself at her and beg her forgiveness. He'd caused both his parents a whole lot of grief and didn't know if either would ever be able to forgive him. Yet here they were.

"Matt, don't just stand there, come help your father out of the car."

He gave a curt nod and strode forward. It took every bit of his self-control to keep his emotions at bay. Up until he'd been accused of murder, they'd been as close as a family could be.

His father had already started to get out of the limo. "Good God, woman, I'm not some ancient invalid. I can still climb out of a car under my own steam."

"I know that, Jacob, but you're exhausted," Evelyn Spalding gently scolded. "Humor me, will you? Matt, please help your father into the…house."

Matt hid a grin. His house was about the size of their pool cabana back in L.A.

Before he'd even taken one step, his mother ran forward and wrapped her arms around him. Matt squeezed her so tight he lifted her off the ground. Tears stung his eyes. "I'm sorry," he whispered. "I never meant to stay away so long, but when you wouldn't speak to me I—"

"Shush. The only people who owe apologies here are your father and I." She stepped back and smiled up at him, a smile he'd missed so much over the months. "Now help your father out of the car before he has another attack."

"Dammit, Evelyn, I'm...fine," Jacob Sr. huffed as he climbed out of the limo. "Just not as young as I used to be. Well, boy, you going to come give me a hug, or do I need to chase you down for one? And I could, you know," he added with a scowl at his wife.

Lindy rushed forward and beat Matt to the punch, throwing her arms around their father's neck. "Daddy, you should be in bed! What were you thinking taking such a long trip?"

"Melinda, let go of your father's neck before he ends up in traction. And it's not as if we drove here, for goodness sake, we took the jet."

Matt watched in amazement as the driver pulled his parents' suitcases from the trunk. "You guys are planning to stay here? In my house?"

"House? That's a generous overstatement," his father teased, eyeing the cottage with a doubtful squint.

Matt ignored the crack and gave him a hug. "I'm very grateful you're all right."

"I know." They shared thumps on the back. "So, you got a beer for your old man?"

"Don't even try it," his mother warned. She grabbed her toiletry bag and followed Lindy into the house.

Matt gave an apologetic shrug. "She's probably right, Dad. No sense chancing your health this soon."

Jacob Sr. scowled. He grabbed two suitcases, no doubt just to prove he could. "How is a man supposed to talk business with his son if he can't even have a drink?"

"Sorry," Matt said, "but you'll have to settle for apple juice or bottled water." After a moment, his father's words sunk in. "Did you say business?"

Jacob Sr. smiled from ear to ear. "Yep. Bought a new one about a month ago. In fact, we can go take a walk through later. It's right here on the outskirts of Redemption."

Chapter Nine

"Son, I thought you'd be happy. You can stay here in Wisconsin with your lady friend, run the new plant. A win-win situation, as they say."

Matt stared at his father, wishing like hell things had turned out differently with Carrie. But opening up the old repackaging plant was a great idea. Matt had heard how bad the economy was in Redemption those first few years after the original plant closed. He loved the thought of bringing so many new job opportunities to the area. Too bad he wouldn't be here to see it.

"My lady friend doesn't want anything to do with me." Matt passed his father a plate with a turkey sandwich on rye and some carrot sticks.

The old man stared at the food as if it would jump off the plate and bite him. "It's good for you," Matt assured him, biting back a grin.

With a sigh of resignation, Jacob Sr. set the plate down and picked up his sandwich. "Might as well be dead if I have to eat this garbage for the rest of my life." He let out a heavy sigh. "So what happened with this Carrie girl?"

"If you know her name, you must know what happened. Now eat your sandwich."

His father cocked a brow. "You're not too old for me to put across my knee. Don't test me, boy." He took a big bite of his sandwich. After swallowing he pressed, "So you're just going to give up? Let her get away?"

Matt picked up his wineglass and drained it. "Don't see how I've got much of a choice. She found out who I am in the worst possible way. Probably thinks I'm some murdering playboy who got off because I'm rich."

"When the hell did you lose your backbone?"

Matt frowned. "Why do you even care? I figured you'd give me some lecture about how she's beneath me, just out for my money, blah-blah-blah."

Jacob Sr. set his sandwich down. "Those first few days after my heart attack I had a lot of time to think, and your mother and I had some long talks in the hospital. Son, I can't tell you how sorry I am for the way we've treated you. I should've been more supportive during that whole actress fiasco instead of worrying about the effect it would have on the company. I also knew you weren't ready to take over the company, but I was being selfish. I wanted to spend the rest of my years golfing, traveling the world with your mother—"

"And who could blame you?" Matt interjected. "Dad, you had every right to want to retire. You've dedicated your life to SI, missing birthdays and anniversaries—"

"That's exactly why I shouldn't have been so eager to push it on you. I hate that I missed so much. I'd give anything to be able to turn back time and attend even one of your little league games."

His father's expression was so solemn Matt didn't know what to say. He'd never seen the old man like this, never knew he felt this way. "Mom was there."

"I should've been there, too. Sitting right beside her, cheering you on."

Matt gave a reluctant nod. "I wish you had been, but I understood. And that was a long time ago, Dad. Don't start punishing yourself now."

The old man picked his sandwich up and considered it. "I just want you to make better choices, son. Learn from my mistakes."

His father looked up just as Matt felt a delicate pair of hands settle on his shoulders.

"And mine," his mother said. "You're my son, and I allowed you to feel guilty for things that had nothing to do with you—like your father's health. I was being selfish. After all those years of eighty hour work weeks, I think I was looking forward to his retirement more than he was."

"Not possible, darlin'," Jacob Sr. teased with a wink.

"So when you informed us you'd changed your mind about taking over," his mother continued, "and planned to go into seclusion for a while...well, we reacted badly, like big babies instead of concerned parents."

Matt turned and gave his mother a kiss on the cheek.

"Well, you're about to get your wish, as belated as it is. I'm ready to take over the company."

Lauren poured Carrie a glass of iced tea and then sat down across from her. Almost immediately, Carrie had regretted her harsh words to Matt. It was just...he'd sworn so many times that she could trust him, and after finally opening herself up—both emotionally and physically—BAM! Turns out he's been lying to everyone since the moment he arrived in town.

But once she'd had some time to cool down and think with her head instead of her heart, she wondered if maybe she'd overreacted. And if she were being honest, the surge of jealousy that tightened her chest after learning Matt had actually dated Amanda Ames may have clouded her ability to think rationally. Heck, why would he want some small-town nobody like her when he could have practically any woman in the world? Out in Hollywood, big boobs—albeit fake—were a dime a dozen.

"Carrie, for what it's worth, I honestly believe that man adores you. It's written all over his face every time he looks at you."

"Then why the lies? Why couldn't he have just told me the truth?"

"Maybe because it's not easy to admit to the woman you care about that you were accused of murdering another."

Carrie took a thoughtful sip of her iced tea. "Love."

"Huh?"

"He told me he loves me. Today, after basically threatening me, he tells me he loves me. Pissed me off something fierce."

Lauren let out a soft chuckle. "Only you would be pissed off over a declaration of love."

Carrie smiled reluctantly. "You did hear the 'threatening me' part, right?"

"Did you threaten him first?"

Lauren knew her so well. "Maybe. I was mad as hell, Laur. But after thinking about it, I just can't figure out any other reason for him to say those words unless...unless he meant them." New hope filled her chest to near bursting. Matt was gorgeous, smart, sexy, rich, and he wanted *her*.

"Carrie," Lauren reached across the table and covered her hand. "Of course he meant it. Caleb knows Matt better than anyone in town and he thinks the world of him. And I trust Caleb's instincts."

"So, what do I do?"

"I think a more important question is, do you love him?"

So much so it hurt. "Yes."

Lauren smiled and winked at her. "Then you wait until he's worked up enough nerve to face you again, and magnanimously forgive him. And while we wait," she added, grinning, "I tried a new pie recipe today—Orange Creamsicle."

Carrie laughed softly. "Sounds like heaven."

By Friday, the work on the coffee shop was complete. The new tables, chairs, and booths had been delivered and installed, the drive-thru window was ready to open. Yet Carrie still hadn't heard from Matt. The contractor assured her everything had been paid in full, but that's all he would say.

Carrie decided to take a drive past Matt's house, and her heart dropped into her stomach with a splash. A For Sale sign was staked in the front yard. She stopped in the middle of the street and gazed at it in disbelief, praying her eyes were playing tricks on her. Realizing her sight was just fine, Carrie squealed her tires in her haste to get away, not caring if she left a block full of people gawking in her wake.

She drove home and parked in her garage, unable to move, unable to breathe. He'd left her. He'd told her he loved her, then left without so much as a "See ya later, it's been fun." The ache in her chest grew until she thought she would suffocate. Tears burned her eyes, and she squeezed them tight, too angry to let them fall. He'd said he loved her, and she'd believed him. Like a damn idiot, she'd believed a rich and powerful man like Jacob Spalding had fallen in love with her. God, what a joke.

Of course, the humiliation she'd felt after seeing her face plastered on every rag mag at the checkout line with captions that read "Jacob Spalding Jr. found in the 'bosom' of small town America" and the like had been bad enough, but at least she'd been able to console herself with the knowledge that Matt loved her—despite the fact he still hadn't called or stopped by. It was simply par for the course when you dated someone from that world.

Now, just thinking about the stories that were sure to follow once Matt was back in circulation was enough to tempt her into packing her bags and moving to Siberia. One thing was for damn sure, though. It would be a cold day in hell before she let another man into her life—or into her heart.

She took a deep, shuddering breath and climbed out of the car. She'd fix herself a sandwich, curl up on the couch, and finish the book she hadn't been able to concentrate on for days. With any luck at all, she wouldn't have to cry herself into an exhausted sleep again tonight.

THE PERFECT BLEND

Armed with a chicken salad sandwich and a can of Pringles, Carrie was about to head into the living room when a movement outside caught her eye. She hurried over to peer out the window. Her plate slipped from her grasp and clattered to the counter. Sitting on the hammock was Matt. He had a bottle of water in one hand and a manila envelope in the other. Carrie hated the anticipation that quickened her pulse. Matt was here...but why? Then it dawned on her. To sell her back his half of the shop. She took a deep breath, gathered her anger around her like a coat of armor, and walked out the patio door.

"Geez, woman, did you take the scenic route home? I've been waiting over an hour—"

"What the hell are you doing here?" The words came out in breathless wonder; she wished she could grab them back and try it again with more outrage.

"We have unfinished business. You didn't think you'd be rid of me that easy, did you?"

He took a sip of his water, and Carrie couldn't decide which she'd rather do, dump it over his head...or kiss him. *Focus, Carrie, he's only here to discuss 'business'.*

"Whatever you have to say, make it quick. I'm pretty busy."

"You were about to eat a sandwich and read a book," he pointed out with a quirked brow.

"You were spying on me? Looking in my window like some friggin' Peeping Tom?"

"Settle down, sweetheart. I just...I needed to see you. I've missed you."

She stared at him, her hands fisted at her sides. He sounded so sincere...but then, he always did. "Whatever. Again, state your business or get the hell off my property."

He grinned and took another sip of his water. "You're pretty sexy when you're mad. Why don't you come sit with me and I'll show you what's in my envelope."

"Why don't you kiss my fat—"

"Watch it, woman. I'll put you over my knee."

She rolled her eyes. "Gee, what a great comeback. I'm quaking with—"

Matt leapt from the hammock so fast Carrie squealed in surprise. And the fool just stood there grinning at her. "Made you jump."

"Oh, my God, what are you, five?"

"I have a present for you. Come here and I'll give it to you." He gave the envelope a shake.

So he'd signed *Coffee To Chai For* over to her. Great. That's what she wanted...right? She strode forward, her chest tight, as if she were on her way to a funeral instead of on the verge of receiving her freedom back. He capped his water and set the bottle on the ground so he could pull the papers out of the envelope. She stopped just close enough to get a whiff of his aftershave. Damn, the man smelled good.

He held out the papers and asked, "So how do you feel about franchising?"

"What?" She snatched the papers from his hand and looked them over. Apparently, he'd bought a business in Madison. Her heart started pounding. Was he purposely being cruel? He knew her ex owned a coffee shop in Madison. "I don't understand."

He smiled as if he'd just handed her the Hope Diamond. "Look at the address. In about a month, *Coffee To Chai For II* will open up directly across the street from your ex's shop. I figure you'll be able to run him out of business in less than a year. Your coffee is ten times better—yes, I tried his—and you'll be a buck cheaper per cup."

"But...I thought you were here to sell me back your half of the shop."

He leaned back against the trunk of the tree. "That would be quite a trick since I don't own half your shop."

She stared at him, sure he'd lost his mind. And then the truth suddenly dawned on her. My God, how could she not have thought of it before? "You signed the papers as Matt Jacobs, so the contract isn't legal and binding."

"Considering you have three attorneys in your immediate family, I'm surprised you hadn't already figured that out."

"I've had a lot on my mind this week." Like missing you so much I could barely think straight.

"I can relate." He straightened away from the tree and took a hesitant step toward her. "I've missed you, Carrie." When she didn't bolt, he closed the distance between them and took her in his arms, squeezing her so tight she could hardly breathe. "When I decided to move to Redemption, I only wanted to escape the madness of my life in L.A.," he said against her cheek. "I'd been suffocating, between the constant hounding of the paparazzi and my parents pressing me to take over the company. I never expected to find the love of my life here."

He pulled back to gaze into her eyes, reaching up to touch her face with reverence. "I love you, sweetheart. The thought of living my life without you scares the hell out of me. Please put me out of my misery and say you forgive me."

Before she could answer, Matt claimed her mouth with hungry impatience and proceeded to kiss her breathless. Carrie melted beneath him like an ice cream cone under the hot sun. She'd been dreaming about kissing him all week—his taste, his smell, his touch. He stroked his hands up and down her back as if he couldn't get enough of her.

Desire coursed through her, scorching every inch of her body. My God, she'd never imagined she could want a man this much—it frightened her on so many levels. But she had one question she still needed answered before she could even think about committing to him. She broke off the kiss with reluctance. He tried to reclaim her lips, but she placed a restraining hand on his chest and gazed up at him. "Why do you have your house up for sale if you plan to stay in Redemption?"

He cupped her face and rested his forehead against hers. "Seemed kind of silly to own two houses when I can only live in one."

Carrie pulled back and frowned. "Two houses? Matt, if you tell me you paid off my house, I swear I'm going to brain you."

He chuckled. "Relax, sweetheart, I know better than that. I bought the tri-level behind you. It's got a huge living room with a fireplace, five bedrooms, so there's plenty of room for the dozen or so kids we're going to have. Oh, and a Jacuzzi in the master bath, and—"

"Matt?"

"Yeah?"

"I love you, too. But three kids is my limit."

He stared at her for a moment, as if he wasn't quite sure he'd heard right. Then he let out a whoop, swung her up in his arms and spun her around in a circle. They collapsed onto the hammock, laughing. After another mind-blowing kiss, Matt told her about his family purchasing the old repackaging plant just outside of town, and how he would slowly start to take over the family business, give his parents some time to travel. But he also still planned to help out with *Coffee To Chai For*, if she'd have him.

Carrie gazed up at him, her heart so full she feared it would burst. "You'll be a local hero, supplying Redemption and the surrounding areas with so many needed jobs."

"I only want to be your hero."

"You already are. Just don't expect me to start calling you Superman."

He grinned. "I wouldn't dream of it. Now hush up and kiss me again. I have a week's worth of missing you to make up for."

"Your wish is my command."

Author's Note

Matt and Carrie were so much fun for me to write. I sure hope you enjoyed their entertaining and often volatile journey. Stacey Joy Netzel and I would love for you to read the rest of the series and fall in love with the characters who've become our friends.

— Donna Marie Rogers

Thank you for reading!

If you enjoyed *The Perfect Blend*, don't forget to leave a review.

Visit Donna's website to sign up for her newsletter for announcements of all New Releases and *exclusive* sales and content!

www.DonnaMarieRogers.com

Up next in the WELCOME TO REDEMPTION series

Grounds for Change

Welcome to Redemption Series
Book 4

STACEY JOY NETZEL

Charlie Russell lived with a secret for fourteen years, but now guilt has pushed him to the breaking point. He meets psychologist Dana McClain and feels an instant connection that has nothing to do with his Great Dane, Sugar, spilling coffee down her shirt. Dana switched to counseling animals because she has a history of becoming too emotionally involved with her clients. She figures she's safe helping Charlie with Sugar's issues, until he reveals his secret and asks for her help. She tries to convince herself it's all about the dog, not the guy, but history has a way of repeating itself.

Excerpt

The other 'parents' collected their 'kids', and when Charlie hadn't come for Sugar by four o'clock, Dana offered to stay with her while Allie went to her line dancing class with her latest flavor of the month. According to Allie, it was very unlike Charlie to not at least call, and Dana dealt with a fresh wave of guilt for her unkind words.

The afternoon with Sugar had proved rewarding, however. The dog was extremely smart, eager to please, and had already caught on to a number of basic commands. If Charlie didn't mind her continuing, Dana anticipated making a lot of progress the next couple days.

She was in the backyard reading a book in Allie's hammock, Sugar lounging in the grass next to her, when the side gate opened and Charlie strode through. Sugar bounded to her feet with an excited yelp. Dana flipped the book down on her chest and watched him greet his dog. That he loved the animal, there was no doubt. Her heart gave a little flutter. It beat faster when his somber gaze lifted to hers.

He'd changed into jeans and a black T-shirt that looked incredible with his dark hair and the faint shadow of stubble on his jaw. She'd always been a sucker for the five o'clock scruffy look. Then again, as evidenced by their first meeting, the man could make anything look good. By the time she'd finished drooling and collected her thoughts, he stood by her side. His dark brown eyes were so serious and intense, her stomach quivered.

"I shouldn't have taken off like that." He raked a hand through his newly trimmed hair. "I'm sorry, I just didn't know how to..."

Dana reached out and clasped his hand hanging at his side. "Allie told me about your sister. If I'd have known, obviously I never would've said what I did."

His fingers tightened on hers. "How could you know? You're not to blame."

She lifted her shoulder. "I still feel awful."

His chest rose and fell with a shaky sigh. Dana maneuvered as best she could on the hammock and once she'd made more room, she tugged so he'd sit down. The contraption swung a bit as he lowered his weight onto it, but he steadied them with his feet before glancing toward the house.

"Where's Allie? She's not mad, is she?"

"Of course not. She had a line dancing class, so I volunteered to stay with Sugar."

"Thanks. I should've called."

"It's okay. I hope you don't mind, but Sugar and I did a little work today. Some basic obedience training."

He'd rested their joined hands on his jean-clad thigh, and now rubbed his thumb across her knuckles. Warmth radiated up her arm and spread through her limbs.

"You didn't have to do that," Charlie said.

"It was fun. She's a great dog—very intelligent. Right, Sugar?" The Great Dane lifted her head from her paws and barked twice. Dana smiled. "See? Two means 'yes'."

Charlie's gaze swung from Sugar to Dana. "Seriously?"

Dana laughed at his priceless expression. "No."

He finally cracked a smile. "You almost had me going, there."

"See that? Somewhere in your subconscious, you actually buy into what I do."

His smile turned to a grimace. "I think my subconscious is the one with the problem. Logically speaking, about Sugar specifically, I know what you do makes sense. I didn't mean to say what I did earlier."

"And the other day?"

"I've got all kinds of excuses for that. Where do you want me to start?"

She pretended to consider. "I should just let you off the hook after everything else, but I have a feeling this could be good."

She used his grip on her hand to pull herself into a sitting position, her bare leg soaking up his heat through his jeans. Once the hammock stopped its crazy swinging, she squeezed his hand and smiled up at him.

"Okay, go."

He chuckled. "Well, see, now that I've had time to go over them in my head, I realize they're all pathetically self-centered."

"Excuses usually are," she agreed.

He looked down, watching as he slowly adjusted his hand until their fingers intertwined. "If it's okay with you then, can I apologize instead?"

"Smart man," she murmured.

His gaze locked with hers and held, except for a one second glance at her lips. He leaned forward, then closer still, until she wanted to grab him and drag him the last few inches that separated her from sure-fire heaven.

Grounds for Change is available now at your favorite bookstore or online retailer.

About the Author

USA Today Bestselling author Donna Marie Rogers inherited her love of romance from her mother. Romance novels, soap operas, *Little House on the Prairie*—her mother loved them all. And though it wasn't until years later Donna would come to understand her mother's fascination with Charles Ingalls, Donna's love of the romance genre is every bit as all-consuming.

A Chicago native, Donna now lives in beautiful Northeast Wisconsin with her husband and children. She's an avid gardener and home-canner, as well as an admitted Halloween fanatic. Her passion to read is only exceeded by her passion to write, so when she's not doing the wife and mother thing, you can usually find her sitting at the computer, creating exciting, memorable characters, fresh new worlds, and always happily-ever-afters.

www.DonnaMarieRogers.com